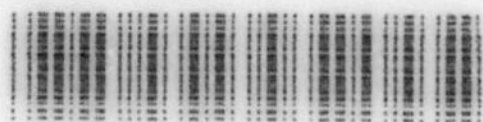

ONE WENT TO DENVER AND THE OTHER WENT WRONG

Crossway Books by
STEPHEN BLY

THE STUART BRANNON WESTERN SERIES

Hard Winter at Broken Arrow Crossing
False Claims at the Little Stephen Mine
Last Hanging at Paradise Meadow
Standoff at Sunrise Creek
Final Justice at Adobe Wells
Son of an Arizona Legend

THE CODE OF THE WEST SERIES

It's Your Misfortune and None of My Own
One Went to Denver and the Other Went Wrong

THE NATHAN T. RIGGINS WESTERN ADVENTURE SERIES
(AGES 9–14)

The Dog Who Would Not Smile
Coyote True
You Can Always Trust a Spotted Horse
The Last Stubborn Buffalo in Nevada
Never Dance with a Bobcat
Hawks Don't Say Goodbye

CODE OF THE WEST

BOOK TWO

ONE WENT TO DENVER AND THE OTHER WENT WRONG

Stephen Bly

CROSSWAY BOOKS • WHEATON, ILLINOIS
A DIVISION OF GOOD NEWS PUBLISHERS

One Went to Denver and the Other Went Wrong

Published by Crossway Books
a division of Good News Publishers
1300 Crescent Street
Wheaton, Illinois 60187

Cover illustration: Larry Selman

First printing 1995

Printed in the United States of America

Library of Congress Cataloging-in-Publication Data
Bly, Stephen A., 1944-
One went to Denver and the other went wrong / Stephen Bly.
p. cm.—(Code of the West; bk. 2)
I. Title II. Series: Bly, Stephen A., 1944- Code of the West series.
PS3552.L9305 1995 813'.54—dc20 94-38680
ISBN 0-89107-834-7

04 03 02 01 00 99 98 97 96 95
15 14 13 12 11 10 9 8 7 6 5 4 3 2 1

For
CARL AND CAROLYN
LIN AND JUDY

1

November, 1882, western Larimer County, Colorado. Sitting cross-legged on the raised wooden front porch, Tap Andrews surveyed the Triple Creek Ranch. In a pile at his left hand were several dozen brass .44-40 casings. With a routine built by years of practice, he scraped each one clean with the small blade of his folding knife and reset a new primer, using the heavy, plierlike reloading tool stamped WCF.

His wide-brimmed, gray sweat-stained hat was pushed to the back of his head. The weathered, leathery wrinkles around his eyes perched above the stubble of a ten-day beard. His boots sported a collection of fall mud and manure.

Glancing across the bare dirt yard, he could see that Brownie and Onespot huddling near the barn had turned their rumps to the cold northwest wind. The sulking, dolorous clouds that had been circling the ranch all day now crouched, anxious to abandon their frozen load.

"Well, fellas," Tap mumbled in the general direction of the two horses, "winter's on its way. This could be that first snowstorm. That's why we got to get some huntin' in. I need meat hangin' in that smokehouse, and I surely don't intend on eatin' my own beef!"

He knew that somewhere back behind the house, stretching up the draw clean to the Wyoming line, were 117 head of longhorn cattle, each packing a freshly burnt Triple Creek brand.

He pushed his smoky-smelling hat back and listened. The trees didn't rustle . . . the stream didn't babble . . . the cows didn't moan . . . the birds didn't chirp. It was as if the whole world had stopped making any sound at all. And in the total silence he thought he heard something.

Scooping the casings into a small cloth sack, he stood up, stretched his six-foot frame, and stepped back into the house. The large, musty front room was dark except for the small blaze of flames from the fireplace. Setting the casing sack on a huge, dust-covered grand piano in the middle of the room, he tramped toward the kitchen, his boot heels slamming the wooden floor and his spurs jingling.

He tore off a wide chunk of sourdough bread and shoved open the back door. A gray and white fur ball flashed into the kitchen and flew toward the living room. "Well, ol' Sal . . . it's surely one of those evenin's for a cat to curl up by the fire, isn't it?"

Sitting at the dining table, he began sliding loaded cartridges into the loops of his bullet belt. The room was almost too dark to see what he was doing, but it was the kind of job Tap Andrews could do in the dark . . . and often did. Finishing the last tough bite of dry sourdough crust, he stood up, brushed the crumbs to the floor, and fastened his holster to his hips. Walking to the front door, he pulled on his heavy brown canvas coat, buttoning only the top button. Then he picked up his Winchester '73. Holding the barrel with his right hand, he draped the stock of the gun back over his shoulder and tugged down the front of his hat.

"Well, cat, I'm ridin' up toward the state line to do a little huntin' before it gets pitch dark, so you keep the fire goin', ya hear?"

Brownie seemed snuffy as Tap rode north. The horse kept prancing, snorting, pulling on the bit, and turning back toward the barn.

"What are you all humped up about?" Tap quizzed. "You think Onespot ought to come and carry home the meat? You might be right. But, shoot, we aren't goin' that far. Now come on, boy . . . settle down . . . just settle down!"

He leaned forward in the saddle to stroke the nervous horse's neck. A blast from the trees east of the corrals sent a bullet sailing over his right shoulder. The brown horse reared on its hind legs. Tap desperately tried to stay in the saddle and jerk his rifle from the scabbard at the same time.

In doing so, he lost his grip on the saddle horn. Feeling the reins slip through his fingers, he tumbled over the cantle and hit the ground on his right shoulder. The horse's panicked kick caught him in the stomach under his left rib cage. Two more shots scattered dust near his head as the horse bolted back toward the barn.

Desperately trying to regain his breath, Tap tried to raise himself to his knees. But the pain in his shoulder and his stomach stunned him for a minute. He couldn't move.

Then he heard someone shout, "Leave the gun in the holster, and jist maybe we won't shoot ya, mister!"

With the wind knocked out of him and pain throbbing in his body, Tap rolled to his back. He lifted himself to his elbows but didn't yank his revolver.

"We're comin' in. You pull that gun, and you're a dead man . . . you understand?" the voice added.

"I kin shoot the eyes out of a squirrel at five hundred yards, mister, so don't go tryin' nothin'!" another voice whined.

Oh, brother . . . there must not be anything but blind squirrels left in Missouri! Every yeehaw with a Springfield claims to shoot squirrels' eyes.

Tap pushed himself up to a sitting position and fought to catch his breath. Finally, he shouted, "Boys, you're makin' a serious mistake. Now it isn't too late to back away. I haven't had to shoot none of you yet."

"We ain't afeared of no gunslinger. We got you from three angles!"

You got me from one angle—the trees. But I'm not sure if my sore right shoulder can lift a gun. Lord, why do things like this keep on happenin' to me?

He could see three men ride out of the ponderosa pines behind the corrals—all pointing their guns at him. Two sported carbines and the other a revolver. There were no sounds other than the creak of old leather and the hoofbeats of the horses. The cold weather kept the mud where he lay stiff enough not to cling to his hands.

"Toss that Colt, and you can stand up, mister!" a gravelly voice shouted.

Tap reached over and grabbed his hat, shoving it back on his head. "Now I just got that Colt cleaned and oiled. I really don't want to go throwin' it in the dirt." He pulled up the slide on his charcoal gray horsehair stampede string.

"We said, throw it down!" an anxious man with a carbine shouted. The voice sounded high-pitched and taut.

Tap slowly pulled out his revolver and flung it into some tall, brown grass about ten feet from where he sat. Then he struggled to his feet.

"You know, boys," Tap drawled, "the years must be seasonin' me. Why, I swear, in the old days I would have just shot you dead and then asked about you later on. But now look at me. Well, I'd sort of like to hear your story first . . . and then I'll shoot you dead."

"You ain't shootin' nobody today, gunslinger! You're dealin' with the Lane brothers from Bolivar, Missouri."

The three riders kept their guns in place and moved their horses toward him. Rubbing his throbbing left shoulder, he shifted his weight to his right foot and studied them as they approached.

The Lane brothers? Whoever heard of the Lane brothers? They're the type that believe everything they read in a dime novel. They'll run. First shot fired their way, and every one of them will run. 'Course, it's tough to shoot when your rifle trotted back to the barn and your Colt's down in the dirt. At least they're predictable. They'll try to circle me.

"It ain't him, Jim-Two. I told you it weren't him!"

The man in the middle riding a long-legged roan spat tobacco to the ground but kept his carbine on Tap.

"Well . . . it's sure that he's somebody, Jim-One . . . and if he's wanted by the law, there's got to be a ree-ward!"

The man rode straight up to Tap, and the other two cut behind him forming a rough triangle.

"Who are you, mister?"

Tap tried to conceal his labored breathing. "Boys, I can't help but feel sorry for ya. The last ones who tried to ambush me in my own place are all planted beneath a mound of Colorado dirt over at Pingree Hill. Except for Beckett, of course. I just buried him out there behind the corral with the horses."

"Beckett? You're the one who brought down Jordan Beckett?" The man called Jim-One gulped.

"Yep."

He's the one. He'll panic.

"I asked your name!"

"Relax, Jim-Two. I told ya he ain't Barranca."

"Shut up, Dusty. I know he ain't that Mexican. Mister, I'll ask you one last time—what's your name?"

"Barranca! You're lookin' for Victor Barranca? Now don't tell me you three are bounty hunters." Tap fought back the pain in his shoulder and tried to crack a smile.

"I told you we was the Lane brothers. That ought to speak fer itself. Do you know Barranca?"

"That lyin', stinkin', cheatin' horse thief? I chased him halfway to Dodge City!" Tap scooted back a few inches as he talked.

This ought to work . . . providin' they don't move sudden-like.

"You ain't goin' to tell us your name?"

"Thanks to you three, my shoulder got thrown out, I got kicked by a horse, and I have three guns pointed at me. Now why on earth should I tell you anything?"

"'Cause we jist might put a bullet in your brain—that's why!" the one riding a sorrel with three white socks sneered.

Jim-Two spat out another chew of tobacco but kept his carbine pointed at Tap. "Don't matter who he is. We'll take him to Denver and see what the U. S. Marshal will give fer him."

The one called Dusty lowered his revolver a little and glanced at the spokesman. "Jim-Two, we ain't headin' back to Denver tonight, are we? This old boy is bound to have some supper in the cabin down there."

Jim-One glanced up at the threatening clouds. "Sure, we could hogtie him to a post and get us a little shut-eye!"

"Start walkin' toward the house, mister," Jim-Two barked.

"I don't think I can make it," Tap protested. "I got kicked pretty good."

"You ain't got no choice!" Jim-One reached over with his carbine and shoved him with the barrel.

Tap staggered forward and then suddenly dove between the legs of the startled sorrel horse, rolled to the tall dead grass, and grabbed his Colt .44. Dusty fired the revolver wildly, and the sorrel bolted with a panicked gallop toward the woods with Jim-One barely able to hold on.

At the same time Jim-Two's horse began frenzied bucking. He dropped the carbine and clutched the saddle horn with both hands. Dusty tumbled off his horse as it reared in the confusion. He squeezed off two more shots as he slammed to the ground, but the bullets tore harmlessly into the dirt.

Tap scrambled across the clearing to the downed man. Grabbing Dusty's thick, greasy brown hair with his left hand, he jammed the blue steel barrel of the Colt into the man's ear. The man reeked of stale beer, campfire smoke, and four months without a bath.

"Dusty, don't think about movin' an eyelid!" Tap commanded. He could feel the man's head quiver and see the sweat bloom on his forehead.

"Don't shoot me, mister," the man pleaded. "Don't shoot me! Please, it was their idee . . . I swear, I told them to go up and make sure it was Barranca."

Tap let the man prattle on but didn't loosen his grip. The shouts and curses from across the clearing caused both of them to glance over at the bucking horse. Two-Jim's saddle had slipped to the right side. For a moment he clutched the horse's mane and then was slung twenty feet into some rocks as the horse spun violently to the right. Stunned, Two-Jim staggered to his feet, took two steps, and then dropped to his face in the dirt. He didn't move.

There was a scream from the woods as One-Jim's horse plowed into the branches, knocking his hapless rider headfirst to the ground.

"You boys definitely need calmer horses if you intend to stay in this line of work. 'Course, it's a little late for that. You won't need a horse where you're goin' now. What made you think that Barranca was out here?" Tap quizzed Dusty.

"Two-Jim . . . It was his idee . . . He . . . eh, he heard from some dance-hall girl over in Pingree Hill that a dark-skinned gunman on the run had moved in out at the Triple Creek Ranch. We figured it was Barranca. Everybody in Durango is lookin' for him. They posted a $1,000 reward to bring him in alive. Don't shoot me, mister . . . I swear, I'll get on my horse and ride out of here and never come back! You cain't shoot me. I dropped my gun. I'm unarmed. Please, mister, please!"

"For pete's sake, stop whining, Dusty!" Tap demanded. "I can't stand a man who snivels. You pulled the gun on me. Now you got to face the music. That's the way the game's played. You knew the rules before you came out here lookin' for trouble."

Dusty rolled his eyes so he could see the cocked hammer on Tap's gun. "What rules? There ain't no rules out here!" he pleaded.

"There's the code," Tap insisted.

"What code?"

"The code that honorable men live by, but I can understand why you've never heard of it."

"We're from Missouri. We don't know nothin'!"

"Well, here's one part—never pull up a chair to the table until you know the house rules. Out here if you shoot at a man, he's got the right to shoot back."

"But . . . but wait . . . Ain't there nothin' in that there code about mercy?" the man begged.

Tap looked at the fear in the man's eyes.

Lord, they come west thinkin' they're playin' a game. Dime-novel desperadoes!

"Get out of here." Tap sighed, releasing the man.

"What?"

"Go back to Missouri and shoot squirrels' eyes, Dusty. Leave the guns on the ground. Get those Jims up off the dirt, catch your saddles, and ride out of here. Every man gets one lucky day in his life. Well, you three used yours up today."

"You ain't goin' to plug me in the back, are ya?"

The scowl on Tap's face caused the man to scamper to his feet and trot over to Jim-Two. After a mumbled conversation, the two men hobbled toward the distant trees and their fallen cohort.

Andrews stood in the clearing until the men were out of sight. Gathering the guns, he hiked back down to the barn. With some effort he pulled himself into the saddle and rode Brownie around the yard to settle him down. His right shoulder ached as he finally pulled the tack off Brownie and turned the horse back into the corral.

"No huntin' tonight, boy! At least . . . not for meat to hang."

He did chores around the yard with the long-range upper tang peep sight flipped up on his '73 rifle until almost dark, keeping a constant eye on the trees behind the corral. Finally a chill slushy drizzle convinced him to retreat inside the cedar-sided ranch house.

In the warmth of the rekindled fire, he examined his wounds.

"Well, Sal," he said nodding at the cat, "you slept through all the excitement. Look at this. That kick from Brownie is going to turn black and blue. And my shoulder is so sore I can't lift my arm above my hat."

He slumped into a straight-back wooden chair next to the fire, stretching his long legs and rubbing his shoulder. Tap kept the Colt holstered at his side. He leaned his head back against the chair and took a deep breath.

Well, Lord, they keep comin'. There's always another, then another, then another. Bounty hunters . . . would-be gunmen . . . and drifters lookin' for some fame. They don't even know who I am, but still they find me. I can't bring Pepper out here to a life like this. I've got to put the past aside before we try to settle down. There's got to be a way to dodge the past.

I'll just ride up to McCurley's tomorrow and have a little heart-to-heart talk. A woman's got a right to something better than this, and I aim to provide it for her.

I'll go down there, and we'll sit in the parlor, and I'll explain it all nice and simple. We'll just postpone things for a while, that's all . . . I mean, it's not like I'm callin' the wedding off.

I'll settle this matter in Arizona first.

Pepper's a good ol' gal. She'll understand. She's done a few things in the past that haunt her too. If there's anyone on earth that can see this plainly, it's Pepper.

"You're what?" Pepper shouted.

"Shhh," Tap cautioned. "There's no reason for everyone at McCurley's to hear."

"You're backin' out, aren't you?" Pepper fumed. "You've been sittin' up there at that big old ranch house plannin' on dumpin' me. You've been leadin' me along, haven't you? Andrews, you ain't nothin' but a lousy, no account, driftin'—"

"Now . . . Pepper . . . listen to me . . . You're not listenin' to me. I just said—"

"Listen to you? I heard all I care to hear, Mr. Tapadera Andrews! You're goin' back to Arizona to find some woman who was crazy enough to shoot her husband because of you."

"That's not what I said! I never mentioned Arizona, and I surely didn't mention Rena!" Tap yelled.

"Don't you yell at me!" Pepper screamed. Out of the corner of her eyes she could see other guests at the McCurley Hotel step to the door of the parlor to watch. "That raven-haired man-killer is still on your mind, is she? Well . . . just . . . just go runnin' back to her. See if I care!" Pepper sobbed.

"Run back to her? What are you yellin' about? I don't want to go back to her. I don't even know where she is! I don't want to ever see her again!" Tap hollered. "Just forget the whole thing. Pretend that I never brought it up. Let's go ahead with the weddin' as planned."

"Wedding? Wedding!" Pepper wailed through the tears. "You think I want to marry you now?"

Tap threw his hat into the green velvet chair. His brown eyes flashed like lightning. "Yes, I do!" He reached out and grabbed Pepper's wrist with his left hand. It felt warm and strong.

"Why should I ever want to marry the likes of you?"

Tap could see Bob and Mrs. McCurley slip through the crowd

and into the parlor. "You'll marry me because I'm crazy about you . . . and I can't stand the thought of living the rest of my life without you . . . and . . . and I love you. That's why!"

He realized that he was shouting at the top of his voice.

"You what?"

Grabbing her by the shoulders, he hollered, "I love you!"

Suddenly Tap realized that it was totally silent in the room. He thought he heard someone behind him clear his throat.

"Oh!" Pepper's teary eyes began to dance as she talked. "That! Well . . . well . . . well, I love you too."

Then she threw her arms around his neck. She could feel the hardened muscles of his arms slip naturally around her waist. Closing her eyes, she pressed her lips against his. As always, they felt warm and wild and comfortable all at the same time.

The applause of the others in the room caused Pepper to pull back and look around wide-eyed. "Haven't you ever seen two people discussin' their weddin'?"

Bob McCurley cleared his throat. "We was just wonderin' whether you two was going to shoot each other or kiss and make up. We was all rootin' for the kissin' part."

McCurley and the others began to step back to the dining room with its aromas of home cooking that filtered into the parlor.

Tap could feel his face flush red with embarrassment. "Eh . . . maybe we should go outside for a little walk."

"It's freezing out there, and that drizzle will make me look like a wet goat." Pepper glanced up into his eyes and then paused. "Yeah . . . maybe you're right. Let me go up and get my wrap."

"I'll wait for you on the porch."

"Cowboy, you're not going to go ridin' off on me, are you?" She ran up the stairs without giving him a chance to reply.

The front porch at the McCurley Hotel wrapped around three sides of the building, with the stairs to the yard facing south. The setting sun was almost completely blocked by the heavy clouds that had sporadically drizzled icy droplets since right before daybreak.

Tap was holding two lap quilts when Pepper met him on the porch wearing a long woolen shawl and tan gloves.

"Did you really want to walk?" he asked her.

"It was your idea as I recall."

"Well, eh . . . what I meant was, let's get some fresh air—"

"And some privacy?"

"Yeah. We could sit here on the bench. The house blocks a little of the drift." Tap laid one quilt across the damp bench and motioned for Pepper to sit down. Once they were both seated, he spread the other over their laps.

"Pepper . . . look . . . I'm sorry I was yelling in there. You had every right to be upset. It's just that I—"

"No," she interrupted, "it was my fault. I just lost control and I—"

"Any woman would have done the same. I know I'm not good at being subtle. I just blurt out things without thinkin' and I—"

"No, no, really," she insisted, "if I would have given you a chance to—"

"Pepper," Tap fumed, "would you please stop interrupting so I can get on with the apology. Our lips will freeze shut before we get anything talked out."

Her troubled eyes silenced him.

Good work, Andrews. Lord, I just don't know how to talk to women right. What am I supposed to do now—apologize for the way I'm apologizing? Maybe some men are meant to stay single!

Suddenly a smile broke across Pepper's face, and she leaned over and pressed her lips against Tap's. Then she pulled back quickly.

But, eh . . . Lord, I'm not one of those men.

"What was that for?" he stammered.

"You seem to be afraid that your lips will freeze. I was merely trying to prevent that from happening."

"Oh . . . yeah . . . well . . . I, eh, I just wanted to talk this thing out with you, and I'm afraid that I'll say something wrong again. But if you'll just bear with me and let me ramble, maybe it will all make sense by the time I'm through."

"All right, Mr. Andrews." She nodded. "That sounds fair enough. And then when you're through, you have to sit here and listen to me."

"That's a deal." He smiled.

"You will let me know if your lips start to freeze shut again, won't you?"

A wide grin sprang across Tap's freshly shaven face. Pepper noticed that his eyes danced as he spoke. "Yes, ma'am. I most definitely will."

"Okay, cowboy, start all over. Tell me why it is you think we should postpone the weddin' until next spring."

"Pepper, ever since I met you I've been tryin' to be a better person. You know that. But you also know it's not easy when you got a past that keeps huntin' you down."

"Is it that trouble in Arizona botherin' you?"

Tap put his right arm softly across Pepper's shoulders.

"Yeah . . . that's the big part. You know that all of this faith stuff is new to me. I don't know much about what God wants out of me, but there's one thing for sure. I've got to do what's right. I was convicted in a court of law and escaped from a territorial prison. I've got to settle that up somehow before I go makin' plans for the rest of my life."

"But you didn't kill that man. You were innocent," she interjected.

"I know that. But the court saw it different. Maybe if I present my case to the territorial governor or something . . . I don't know, Pepper, but it nags at me. Day and night it turns over in my mind, and then some ragtag bountymen like this Lane bunch show up and remind me that I'm still on the dodge."

Pepper raised her right hand up to Tap's and slipped her gloved fingers into his. "But you can't go ridin' down to Arizona. They'll lock you back in Yuma before you ever see the governor or anyone else."

"Yeah, they'll either do that or hang me on sight."

"That's exactly why you've got to stay out of Arizona. I don't think the Lord wants you to serve time in jail for a crime you didn't commit," she countered.

"It wouldn't be the first time a man had to do that." He nodded. "I read about Joseph in the Bible."

"But that was . . . that was . . . you know . . . different. Wasn't it?"

"Yeah . . . well, maybe." He sighed.

They both sat silent for several minutes.

Pepper dropped her hand back on top of the lap quilt and turned to face Tap in the shadows. "If you go back to Arizona, I'll go with you."

"Oh, no. You can't do—"

"Look, Tap, if you're going to go to jail, at least I can live near you and come visit you or something, can't I?"

"It could be dangerous. They'll likely have a dead or alive reward on my head."

"It doesn't matter to me. The day they kill you will be the day my heart dies," she murmured. "It wouldn't be fair to have me sit here and wonder what's happened to you."

Tap glanced at her green eyes. Like a magnet, they always drew him toward her. Finally he looked down at his boots.

"But I can't drag you down there. It's still a violent land. I'd be worried about you night and day."

"It's not exactly peaceful around here. Tap . . . if I told you that I had some dangerous past business to take care of up in Idaho, and I might not be back for several months or years, and I insisted upon going up there by myself, would you let me go alone?"

"Of course not! But that's not the same at all!" His voice began to rise, and he dropped his arm back to his side.

"Why?" she pressed.

"Well . . . because you're a woman, that's why. You could get hurt and . . . and . . ."

"And what?"

"Well, I'd be so worried sick about you I wouldn't be worth two cents!" he fumed.

"And that's exactly how I'd be if you go to Arizona without me."

Tap sat there for a minute. Then he slipped his hand back into hers. "You're right. If I go to Arizona, you're coming with me."

"If?" she questioned. "You have doubts about it?"

"I never said I was goin' for sure. I just want to see if I can get this thing cleared up."

"So what is your plan?"

"Look at that!" He motioned to the yard. "It's turning into snowflakes." He turned the collar of his coat up and snuggled closer to Pepper. "You want to go in?"

"Not yet. How about you?" she asked. "You gettin' cold?"

"Well, eh . . . only my lips." He grinned.

Pepper's lips felt soft and warm as they brushed against his. "Now, cowboy, what kind of plan do you have?"

Tap struggled to regather his thoughts. "I thought I'd try to talk to Stuart Brannon. He's got a lot of pull down there, and maybe we could sit down with the governor together."

"Brannon? I thought you said he was the one who brought you in."

"Yeah, but he's about the only man I know personally that will give a man an honest shake. He knows I'm innocent, I think."

"So we're goin' to ride down to Arizona and take our chances?"

"Nope."

"But I thought you said—"

"I said I needed to get hold of Brannon. I figure on writin' him a letter to see if we can meet—say in Utah or Nevada—and discuss the matter."

"What's to keep him from bushwhackin' you and takin' you back to Arizona for the reward money?"

"Not Brannon. He won't do that sort of thing for money. And if he gives you his word . . . Well, he's the only man I know who could walk into any bank in the territory and borrow every last dollar in the safe just on his word. No, if he agreed to sit down and talk, I wouldn't have to worry."

"If all you're goin' to do is write a letter, why did we have this big argument? I thought you said you had to go someplace, be gone for weeks and weeks, and settle the matter."

"Well, I do, sort of. I've got a friend in Denver. You ever heard of Wade Eagleman?"

"Is he a shootist?"

"Nope. He's an attorney. Wade and I go way back. We came up the trail together one spring with Charlie Goodnight. Wade's about two-thirds Comanche, but he's also one of the best lawyers in the state. I'll slip into Denver and look up Wade. He can send Brannon a telegraph. We'll make it all legal-like."

"So all you've been sayin' is that you want to take a trip to Denver to see some attorney? Tap Andrews, if you would have said that in the first place, there wouldn't have been any problem at all."

"I figured I might just stay in Denver until Wade gets word back. Maybe it would mean ridin' down to Arizona. Maybe not. That's why I figured we'd need to put the weddin' on the shelf until later. But if you're goin' with me, we could always—"

"Goin' with you?"

"Sure, you talked me into lettin' you come along."

"I ain't goin' to Denver. I thought you were talking about Arizona." She sat straight up and pulled back from Tap.

"What? We've been through all that. You said—"

"I never said I'd go to Denver. There's no way you're getting me to Denver."

"But . . . but . . . you just told me that—"

"Tap Andrews," Pepper declaimed, her voice rising, "I told you I am not now, nor will I ever go to Denver!"

"What happened in—"

"I'm not talking about it, so you can just change the subject, thank you!"

"Now you're the one who's not makin' any sense," he boomed.

"Don't you start yellin' at me again!"

"When you start makin' sense, I'll stop yellin'!" he shouted. The fog from his breath floated like smoke across the porch.

"I can't go back to Denver. And that's final."

Tap tried to lower his voice. "But what happened in—"

"I'm not telling you now. I'm not telling you ever!" she insisted. "There are some things that best remain hidden. I don't want you to ever ask me about Denver!"

Tap heard her voice start to quiver, but he didn't see any tears.

"But I might be there several weeks."

"It don't matter . . . I can't go," she persisted.

"But what if I get word that Brannon will meet with me? I might not have time to come back out here and get you."

"Send word by stage, and I'll meet you in . . . in Durango or Santa Fe or wherever. But I'm not going to Denver."

They sat silent in the darkness until Mrs. McCurley tapped on the window pane behind them and motioned them to come in before supper was all gone.

"I won't go to meet Brannon without you." Tap stood up and helped Pepper to her feet.

"You promise?"

He nodded. "My word's good."

"As good as this man Brannon's?"

"Eh . . . I hope so."

"Can you walk into any bank in the territory and borrow every last dollar with nothing more than a promise?" she teased.

"Only if I have a gun in my hand and a bandanna over my face."

"I'll worry about you the whole time you're in Denver," she confided.

"Well, you better." He smiled. "'Cause I'll be anxious about you the whole time too."

"There isn't any need for that. I'll just be up in my room pinin' away for some no-account, driftin' gunman."

"I thought you were goin' to be thinkin' about me," he kidded.

Tap jumped back to miss her swinging right arm and raked his spurs across the wooden porch. "You are the no-account!" she hollered.

"Well, I'll worry about you anyway. Some smooth-talkin', rich mine owner might pull up here in a big black buggy and talk you into movin' into his mansion."

"Are you really worried about losin' me?"

"Yep."

"Good."

"Why?"

"'Cause it will give you a reason to hurry back to McCurley's."

"I'm surely not goin' to stay in Denver one day longer than I need to. I want to get back before the passes snow in for the winter. Do you want me to bring you anything from Denver?"

Pepper's eyes began to sparkle. "Oh . . . yes! Bring me some cream-colored satin and matching lace, mother-of-pearl buttons, and some thread and—"

"Whoa! Write all of that down for me. How in the world am I going to pick out stuff like that?"

"Oh, I'm sure a millinery shop will be able to fill the order. Just give them the list."

They walked toward the front door of the hotel.

"Now let me get this straight." Tap paused before they reentered. "We argued up and down about whether I was to go off and finally decided I should go and you should go with me. Only now you aren't goin' because you had a bad experience in Denver once?"

"I had a living nightmare in Denver. Sometimes I still wake up screaming. But I don't want to talk about it."

"Well," Tap sighed, "maybe we better get to that supper. It's gettin' a might cold out here."

She winked. "Are your lips cold again?"

Brushing his callused hand over his slightly chapped lips, he grinned. "Yes, Miss Pepper, these lips are absolutely freezing. What do you suppose I should do about it?"

"Well, Mr. Andrews, if I were you, I'd march right in there and have a big bowl of Mrs. McCurley's soup!"

Pepper spun on her heels and entered the hotel.

2

An inch of fresh, wet snow dusted the yard as Tap Andrews stood in the doorway of McCurley's barn with his bedroll over his shoulder. A slight crack in the heavy clouds pressing up against the Rocky Mountains caused the early morning eastern sky to take on a rose and purple color. The air was damp, frigid—yet clean.

Brownie walked stiff-legged as Tap led the horse out of the stalls to the hitching rail in front of the hotel. Tap yanked on the latigo and retied it, leaving the reins looped over the saddle horn. With a small stick in hand he circled the horse, lifting each hoof to check the frog for stones and mud.

For Tap the aroma of horseflesh and saddle leather was the smell of leaving. He glanced up at Pepper's upstairs window but couldn't see any light in her room.

Lord, it seems like I've spent my whole life leavin'. I guess a man doesn't remember the "howdys" as much as the "so longs." Well, darlin', I surely hope I know what I'm doin'. Sometimes doin' the right thing takes a lot of figurin'. Now doin' wrong . . . that takes no thought at all. I'm goin' to miss you. I'll miss that smile . . . and those eyes . . . and . . . and those sweet, soft lips.

"Are you goin' to stand there in the snow gawkin' up at my window all day or what?"

"Pepper!" Tap turned toward the front door of the hotel to see her wrapped with a quilt around her bathrobe and her wavy blonde hair combed down past her shoulders. "I, eh . . . didn't think you were up yet."

"Well, I'm not. I'm sound asleep. I surely don't get up at this time of the day for just any old no-account drifter."

"Thanks. I was startin' to miss you already."

"You aren't goin' to be gone all that long. Just pretend you're burnin' hair on them old longhorns or something. Here, I made you up a grub sack."

Pepper handed him a heavy packed flour sack.

"What are you going to be doin' 'til I get back?" he asked.

"Mrs. McCurley's hired me to help with some of the cookin'. I do know how to cook, you know."

"You're goin' to get up and cook breakfast?"

"I didn't say breakfast. My job will be to help with dinner and cook supper."

Tap stepped up on the porch and took the food sack. "Are you barefooted? You'll freeze out here barefooted," he chided.

"It ain't my toes that is cold." She grinned.

"Well, if your ears are cold, perhaps you should wear—"

"It ain't my ears neither. Cowboy, it's my lips that is freezin'!"

"Well," Tap exclaimed, "if I were you, I'd hustle right in there and have a nice, hot cup of coffee!"

"And it's a good thing I ain't you," she fumed as she threw her arms around him and kissed him.

Tap figured the soft, warm feel of the kiss lasted just over the first hill east of McCurley. There a frigid northern wind caused him to tighten the stampede string on his hat and turn his collar up.

The further he rode up the trail to the east, the lower the clouds seemed to hang. By noon he and Brownie were in a dripping, freezing fog that left his clothes soaked and his eyes stinging. He had just built a fire on the south side of the trail when a carriage drove up from the east.

"You boys are welcome to noon it with me," Tap called as they paused and waited for him to signal them in.

"Much obliged, mister. It's a miserable time to be comin' over the pass. Yes, sir, a warm fire will take some chill out of my bones." The lanky man spoke with a slowness of speech formed by years of working long cattle drives . . . or being on the run.

Climbing out of the carriage, the two men joined Tap at the fire.

"Help yourself to some grub." He motioned.

"We got our own fixin's, but a cup of that coffee would be nice. They call me Pardee, and this is—"

"He doesn't need my name!" grumbled the big man with a thick mustache and gray hair at the temples.

"Nope." Andrews sipped coffee from his blue-enameled tin cup. "But you can call me Tap."

"I suppose this is about the right time of the year for this snow. 'Course, I'd like to see it wait 'til after Christmas. I remember one year the passes snowed up by the middle of October . . . that was six, seven years ago, I reckon." Pardee continued to jabber while Tap and the other man sized each other up.

He probably carries a sneak gun and a knife. And that Colt ain't parked on his hip just for looks. He's the kind that thinks he's suppose to win every hand he draws.

"You all headin' on west a spell?" Tap finally asked.

"Where we're traveling is none of your business," the big man snapped.

"Oh, don't mind him. Yep, we're goin' west." Pardee nodded. "I hear a man kin catch a room at the McCurley Hotel. Is that right?"

"Yep. McCurley's got a nice little hotel there. "'Course, he's a God-fearin' man who don't put up with no slack, if you catch my drift."

"Well, on a day like this one, all we need is a dry bed and meal. We aim to try and locate an old friend out that way," Pardee added. "Can we get there by dark?"

"You'll have to push it in this weather. I don't figure there's enough daylight left," Andrews instructed him. "But the hot apple pie is worth the effort. You might not be too late for supper. Mrs. McCurley will stir you up something if you got the fare."

"Now that sounds mighty fine. It's got to beat that supper we had last night." Pardee pulled some jerky out of his grub sack.

"You stopped at Pingree, I reckon," Tap remarked.

"Yep." Pardee grinned. "Oh, the likker and girls is fine, but that big old boy who cooked breakfast this mornin' burnt them eggs harder than the streets of Denver."

"That must be Stack. He's a good man to the bone." Tap cracked a smile. "But he isn't a cook. Grab another cup of coffee 'cause I've got to load up and be on my way. If this thing cuts loose and starts snowing, I'll never make it through the mountains."

"Thanks, mister." Pardee nodded. "And if you stop at April's dance hall, don't eat them eggs."

Tap cinched up Brownie and loaded his gear. Mounting up, he swung back by the men at the fire before he rode up to the trail.

"Thanks again for the fire," Pardee called. "Take her mighty careful up there. You're headin' into the teeth of this thing."

"Well, Pardee . . . I hope you make it to McCurley's. But frankly I wouldn't travel with a man who keeps one hand always attached to a sneak gun in his coat pocket." He nodded at the bigger man.

"He what?" Pardee looked over at the other man.

"Yeah, I couldn't decide if he wanted to kill me . . . or you."

"What's he talkin' about, Dil—"

"I thought you were leavin', mister!" the nameless man gruffed at Tap.

"I aim to do just that. Well, Pardee, watch your back . . . and I hope you find that pal of yours out there," Tap called.

"Pal?" Pardee laughed. "We ain't lookin' for a pal. We're lookin' for a gal."

"Shut up, Pardee. You talk too much!" the other man snapped.

Pardee reached for his revolver. Then he backed off and shrugged.

Andrews pushed Brownie up the steep trail.

"Well, old boy, at least they got the drift at their back this afternoon. We'll be headin' right into it. If they're lookin' for a gal, they should have stayed at April's. Seems to me those two will be at each other's throats long before they get there."

The clouds lifted to the treetops about midafternoon, and it began to snow. It wasn't a heavy snow—just scattered flakes, each about the size of a two-bit piece and each packing drops of water. Tap's ducking trousers were soon soaked, his jacket was getting heavy, and his hat began to droop.

His deerskin gloves began to hold water, and he debated whether it would be warmer to cram them back into his saddlebags. It was too blustery and cold to stop and talk with any of the other travelers he met on the road. All seemed content to tip hats and keep moving.

It was after dark when Andrews thought he saw a flicker of kerosene light off to the left. He trotted over and came up in front of April Hastings's dance hall.

Dropping Brownie's reins to the snow, he stepped up to the porch and peeked inside the door.

"Hey, piano man, is this a funeral?" Tap called.

The strong-shouldered, tall man at the piano stool spun toward the door.

"Tap! Did you get lost in this storm?"

"Now that's a fine greeting, Stack. I ride all this way just to taste your fine cowboy cuisine, and you chide me like that."

Stack ambled over and threw his arm around Tap's shoulder. "Come on in . . . we've got three old boys passed out in the back of the saloon, but other than that, the place is empty. April's told the girls they can stay upstairs if things don't pick up. You're stayin' with us, ain't ya?"

"I was hopin' to sleep out in the barn. I've got to put up my pony."

"Shoot, Tap, you can stay in here . . . eh, in my room. You know that."

"Stack, if Pepper found out I spent the night at April's, it would be a mighty fierce fight. You know what she can do."

"Yep. I reckon it would be like cornerin' a wolverine in the woodshed. Well, let me get a lantern and walk you out. You need some coffee? You're soakin' wet! I kin rustle you up some eggs."

"Eh . . . no thanks, Stack. I just need a soft spot and some warm blankets."

The two men stepped out into the storm. The flickering lantern twinkled off the falling snow. If he hadn't been half frozen, it would have been a beautiful sight. By the time Tap had Brownie stalled for the night, Stack had the little wood stove in the calving room crackling with burning pine.

"How's Pepper doin', Tap?" the piano player and saloon bouncer asked. "I still haven't got my invitation yet."

"Pepper's doin' great. You ought to see her helpin' out around McCurley's—sewin', cookin', and the like. She's actin' more like an eastern gal every day."

"But you didn't mention the weddin'," Stack prodded. "You two are still agreed on that, ain't ya?"

"You know," Tap said with a grin, "that girl can be one of the most stubborn, pigheaded—"

"The weddin'?" Stack interrupted.

"Oh . . . well, it will be comin' up shortly. Don't worry. You're still goin' to be the best man. But it'll probably be spring."

"I thought she wanted a Christmas weddin'."

"Well, I figure . . ." Tap paused. "To tell you the truth, Stack, I need to take care of some Arizona business before I settle down up here."

"You got a ranch down in the Territory?"

"Not hardly. I got a little legal problem, if you know what I mean."

"Arizona's a long way from here."

"It nags at me on the inside, Stack. You ever had that happen?"

"Sort of." Stack stood up and tossed another stick in the wood stove. "So are you headed to Arizona?"

"Not yet. I need to go into Denver and talk to a lawyer friend of mine. Maybe I can get this taken care of without goin' back south."

"Denver? You headin' over the pass to Denver tomorrow?"

"Unless this storm settles in, I am."

"Well, shoot, I need to go get some winter supplies. Mind if I bring the wagon along with you?"

"I'd enjoy the company, Mr. Lowery." Tap grinned.

"That's mighty fine, Tap. I was kind of dreadin' that trip alone. We'll roll out in the mornin' . . . after I cook you them eggs."

"Eh . . . well, we ought to hit the trail early and try and beat the snow," Tap suggested.

"Oh, a man's always got time for some ham and eggs. Well, I've got to get back over to the dance hall and wake them drifters up so I can throw them out on their ears. They wore out their welcome and their wallets hours ago."

"Where they from?"

"Can't tell you that, but they were in here the other night. You want to hear something comical? All three is brothers, you know. The oldest goes by the name of Jim-One, and the second one is called Jim-Two. Now don't that seem—"

"And Dusty?" Tap groaned.

"You know them boys?"

"They tried to yeehaw me a couple days ago at the ranch, and I had to run them off."

"You want me to hogtie 'em? I don't think they have more than one gun between the three of them."

"They aren't worth the effort. Just toss them out the door and tell 'em some old boy from the Triple Creek Ranch is in the barn threatenin' to shoot them on sight."

"Won't they try and jump ya?" Stack asked.

"I don't think so. You tell them that, and they'll be halfway to Missouri by daylight."

Tap kept a fire burning in the calving shed stove. He hung out most of his clothes to dry. Leaving the shed door open, he climbed the ladder and spent the night in the loft, half-buried by hay, his Colt .44 in his right hand. The soft, sweet smell of hay and the security of being where no one would think to look for him helped him sleep soundly.

Daylight had not broken yet when he pulled his dry, stiff clothes on and began to saddle up Brownie by the light of a flickering lantern.

Lord, this is Tapadera Andrews talkin', and I'm headed toward Denver. Now I don't really know what will happen there. It's just . . . Well, I got a wrench down deep in my belly—kind of like when a man's real hungry. You know what I mean? I got to take care of it. I know I'm not very seasoned at this sort of thing . . . so, eh . . . stick with me and I'll try to learn. I know You'd want—

"Hey, *compadre!* I figured you roust out early." Stack burst into the barn carrying two tin plates. "This is your lucky day, *amigo*. My specialty—a chili omelette!" Stack shoved an enameled tin plate of smoldering black and green stuff at Tap.

"Eh . . . well, I was not too, eh . . . maybe I should just—"

"No need to thank me. I was goin' to stir some up for me and Selena anyway."

"Selena's up already?" Tap finally shoved a bite of the eggs into his mouth and turned away from Stack as he ate.

"The girls all turned in early last night. No one wanted to ride through that storm to come to the dance hall. But I see stars out there this mornin', so maybe it will be clear for a while."

Tap cinched down the saddle and tied his bedroll onto the cantle as he tried to swallow another bite of rancid, bitter, burnt, slick, almost unchewable eggs. "How's that Selena doin'?" he managed to mumble.

"She's been sailin' ever since Pepper moved out and you buried that Beckett gang. She's sort of the center of attraction now, and a dance hall only needs one queen bee. I think she's countin' on you sayin' hello before we ride off."

"Well, I'm ready to pull out. You need some help hitchin' up that wagon?"

"Nah," Stack insisted. "Go on and greet Selena and eat them eggs. You don't want them to get cold. They don't taste so good when they're cold."

Tap left Brownie in the warm barn and stepped out into the cold, crisp early morning air. A thin gray line in the east announced the approach of daylight. His boot heels crunched in the shallow layer of frozen snow. He was still chewing on a bite of eggs and carrying his plate when he reached the side door that led directly to the kitchen.

A bathrobe-wrapped woman with waist-length, thick black hair and flashing dark eyes swung open the door.

"*¡Caballero!* My hero . . . come in, come in!" She smiled.

Tap stepped into the stuffy, sweet-smelling kitchen and looked at her in the flickering lantern light.

"Ai, yai, yai, Señorita Selena. You are more beautiful than all the roses in San Antonio!"

"Sure, and Stack's a great cook!" she laughed. "Do you really eat those things?"

"Eh . . . don't you?" Tap questioned.

"Are you kidding? I give 'em to the cat."

"I don't see a cat." Tap searched the room.

"Nah, he ran off. Can you blame him? How you doin' anyway, cowboy?"

"Good . . . I'm doin' good."

"And Pepper? How's that blonde wildcat? Did she tear out your hair or try to knife you?"

"Selena, you don't ever give up, do you?" Tap grinned.

"Nope. But I do envy her."

"There are other men around—"

"Oh, I don't envy her because she got you. You ain't all that much really. But she got out at a good time. Business has been bad, and the type of men that's movin' in ain't nearly as considerate as that old bunch."

"I thought the old bunch was pretty rotten."

"That should tell you something about these new ones."

"Well, I hear Stack rollin' that wagon into the yard, so I better pull on out. I didn't want to leave without sayin' hello."

Selena took his tin plate and spun back toward the sink. "You just wanted to get rid of them horrible eggs, that's all." She laughed.

"*Hasta la vista*, Selena."

"*Hasta que nos enamoremos*, Señor Tapadera Andrews."

The cold morning air felt especially brisk on his flushing face and neck. He pulled down his gray felt hat and tried to think of Pepper.

"You get enough to eat?" Stack hollered from the wagon.

"Yep." Tap called back as he rode Brownie out of the barn. "I don't figure I could eat another bite!"

After three cold, clear, uneventful days Tap and Stack rolled into Denver. The streets were mostly frozen over. The wooden sidewalks were dirty and crowded, and no one looked up as they drove into town. Tap rode on the wagon with Stack, and Brownie was tied to the back of the rig.

"This place looks busier than ever," Tap remarked. Crowds of men huddled at almost every corner of the city. "'Course, I haven't been here in a few years."

"It's that big old thing Tabor and Loveland put on last summer that stirred everyone up," Stack explained.

"What thing?"

"Oh, you know, old Horace Tabor and William Loveland organized that National Mining and Industrial Exposition. You heard about that, didn't you?"

"Eh . . . no, I don't guess I did."

"Where you been, boy?" Stack chided. "In prison?"

"I guess it wasn't newsworthy in Yuma."

"Well, lots of them eastern tourists and visitors just up and decided to stay. There's been boomers, boosters, and land speculators on every corner ever since."

"She's grown a lot since I was here last."

"Where are you goin' to find this guy Eagleman?" Stack asked.

"Where's the biggest poker game in town?"

Stack pulled the wagon onto a side street and parked it next to the wooden sidewalk. "That would be at the Front Range Club . . . but watch out for them. Many a rich man has walked out of there stone-broke."

Tap climbed back to the wagon's tailgate and unhitched Brownie. "Don't worry, I'm not going there to play poker. I'm tryin' to find Wade Eagleman. If he's not in court, he'll be playing poker . . . or dead. How about you, Stack? Where you plan on stayin'?"

"I'm goin' to go see my baby sister. She just got married last summer. Then I'll go buy supplies."

"Your sister? I didn't know you had a sister."

Stack grinned. "I got seven sisters!"

"Seven! And they're all younger than you, right?"

"How'd you know that?"

"Just a guess." Tap climbed aboard Brownie. "I'll probably stay at the Drovers' . . . if it hasn't burned down by now. If I don't see you around town, I'll stop by April's on my way back out to the ranch."

"You know you're always welcome to stop a spell. April and the girls would enjoy your company."

Tap sat in the cold saddle and watched as Stack rambled up the street lined with small, unpainted houses and leafless trees.

Seven sisters? Lord, he's spent his entire life takin' care of girls. Surely there's some kind of heavenly reward for that.

It took Tap over an hour to find the Front Range Club. It turned out to be a two-story brick building with a small brass sign and a locked oak-and-etched-glass front door.

He banged on the glass.

A tall man in a long, black coat and silk tie finally opened the door. He sported sideburns that ran almost to the point of his chin. Tap could tell that he was wearing a Colt on each hip under the coat.

"This is a private club," the man announced. "Members only."

"Wait. I don't want to come in. I just want to get a message to one of your members," Tap called out as the door began to close.

"If you'll write it down, I'll be happy to deliver it." The man closed the door and then reappeared, handing Tap a silver tray with a sheet of paper and a pen.

Quickly, Tap scratched out a note and gave the tray to the man.

"If you'd just give that to Mr. Eagleman, I'll wait out here for a reply," Tap offered.

The man with hidden Colts looked startled. "Mr. Wade Eagleman?"

"Yeah, I just need—"

"I've never heard of him!" the man fired back. Then he wadded the note and tossed it to the steps without reading it.

"But . . . I—" The door slammed shut.

You may not want to talk about it, but you obviously know Wade!

Tap pounded with impatience on the oak-framed door.

There was no answer, but through the opaque etched glass he could see the shadow of someone standing there.

"Go away, or I'll be forced to summon the authorities!" the man shouted.

"Open the door, or I will bust the glass out and come in on my own!" Tap hollered back.

Standing to the side out of sight, he quietly grasped the black iron door handle with his left hand and slipped his Colt from his holster with his right. With the barrel of the revolver he hammered on the oak.

As he heard the faint sound of the latch being unlocked and felt the door begin to open, Tap violently jerked it forward. The man inside, still holding the door handle, staggered off balance to the top outside steps. In his left hand he carried a short-barreled .45, but he was so startled that the gun merely hung to his side.

The barrel of Tap's gun cracked into the man's wrist, and the .45 tumbled onto the granite steps, firing on impact. The bullet ricocheted wildly off the steps and into the street. A crowd of onlookers gathered.

Tap grabbed the man by the collar and yanked his head down waist high, shoving the cold barrel of the.44 into his temple before he had time to pull the other gun.

"Let's try this again, mister!" Tap growled. "Where can I find Wade Eagleman?"

"What's goin' on here?" a man in the crowd shouted.

"No problem," Tap called back. "He forgot to properly cover his bet, that's all."

Tap turned back to the man in his grip and muttered under his breath, "How about it, Mr. Doorman? Where's Wade?"

"I've never heard of the man in my life," came the obviously pained reply. "He is not now, nor has he ever been a member of the Front Range Club."

Tap shoved the barrel harder into the man's face.

"However, if I did know him . . . which I don't . . . I would suggest you look in the jail."

"Jail? At the courthouse? You mean he's got a trial goin' on?"

"I mean," the man huffed, "that if I did know him, I would say he is either locked up behind bars or hung."

"Hung?" Tap released the man, who quickly gathered up his gun, shoved it in his holster, and retreated behind the etched-glass door.

Tap dropped his own revolver back in the holster and scooted through the crowd to where Brownie was hitched. He had turned back toward the street when he heard a shout from the sidewalk.

"Mister, are you lookin' for that half-breed Eagleman?"

Spinning in the saddle, he saw a white-bearded man wave his hat. Tap rode over to the man.

"You know Wade, old-timer?"

"You a friend of his?"

"Yep."

"Well, Eagleman stood by me in court when I didn't have a penny to my name."

"What's this about him being arrested or something?"

"That's right. They claim he shot Crawford Billingsly in the back."

"The railroad man?"

"That's the one." The old man shuffled his feet and shaded his eyes from the sun.

"Wade wouldn't shoot anyone in the back," Tap protested.

"I know that, but they dug up some witnesses who said he done it, and it seems like there is high-up folks who want to see him hung in an awful big hurry. I hear he's sittin' in a jail cell."

Tap sat back straight in the saddle. "Well, thanks, professor." He tipped his hat.

"Hey, mister . . . there's plenty of folks around town that thinks Eagleman's gettin' a raw deal. If you need some help, you might be surprised how many would answer the call."

"I'll remember that," Tap called as he rode Brownie south along the street.

In room 24 on the second floor of the Drovers' Hotel, Tap Andrews lay in the shadows on a lumpy mattress, spinning the cylinder of his Colt.

Lord, if I go marching into the jail to see Wade, someone might recognize me and toss me in there before I get a chance to do any talkin'. Now You know I intend on clearin' up this matter, but I don't plan to get shipped back to Yuma without explainin' my case to someone. Maybe I could just send Brannon a telegraph myself. That way I wouldn't have to depend on Wade or nobody.

'Course, that doesn't help Wade.

Lord, I can't help him. It won't do him no good for me to barge down there and get tossed in with him. 'Course, maybe no one in Denver's ever heard of Tap Andrews. Anyway, if I can't help, I should stay completely away . . . right?

One hour later, wearing a newly purchased dark suit, fancy vest, boiled shirt, and black tie, Tap Andrews sat in the front office of the Denver Jail.

Lord, I feel like an undertaker . . . but I'm not sure whose funeral I'm at. These clothes are bad enough, but not packin' a gun . . . Lord, I figure there must be a dozen men in this town who would try to shoot me on sight if they spotted me unarmed. This is crazy. I shouldn't—

His thoughts were interrupted when a jailer motioned for him to follow. The dark corridor smelled of tobacco, whiskey, and sweat.

"I'll give you ten minutes to make your private arrangements. Do not move your hands toward the prisoner or attempt to take anything from him," the guard droned.

Wade Eagleman looked happy to see Tap but didn't say anything until the guard had retreated.

"Tap! *Compadre* . . . you look like a bull at a ballet. That gold-braided vest is awful!"

"Well, I feel a whole lot worse than I look," Tap complained. "But you aren't exactly doin' so well yourself."

Eagleman dropped his smile. "Yeah . . . look at this. Last time we were together, you were in here, and I was out there. I heard you got hung down in Arizona, but I knew better."

"I was doin' time in A. T. P., but I'm on . . . eh . . . a vacation."

"Who was the woman this time?" Eagleman chided.

"It doesn't matter," Tap muttered. "What can I do to get you out of here?"

"Tap, they pushed this case through in four days. No one's interested in the truth. They just wanted the matter solved. It doesn't look to me like I have a prayer."

"I've already done that."

"What?"

"Pray for you."

"Are you kiddin' me?"

"Nope."

"Man, it has been a long time since we've seen each other."

"What did the notorious trial lawyer and pride of the Comanche Nation do to deserve this?" Tap pressed.

"You ever heard of Crawford Billingsly?"

"Yep."

"Well, we were playin' a pretty high game of draw poker a few months back. I put up twenty lots I own on the north side of town. He decided to answer in kind and put up twenty lots he owned on the next street over from mine. I won the hand on queens and jacks. When he sent me the deeds to the lots, they were for some south side property that isn't worth a third of those uptown lots.

"Well, I pitched a fit, threatenin' to take him to court no matter how rich he was. Anyway, this argument went on and on, week after week. Finally I filed a lien against those good lots and discovered that he had sold 'em all in September!"

"Nice fellow."

"Needless to say I was a little hot under the collar when I saw him at the club."

"The club?"

"The Front Range Club. I'm a member there, you know."

"No, I didn't know that."

"Yeah, it's surprising how money changes the color of one's skin. Anyway . . . he and I fell into a shoutin' match at the club. I got all steamed up and go to saying some things I shouldn't have said."

"I don't suppose you mentioned putting a bullet through his belly at the first chance you got?"

"Or words to that effect. Anyway, that night he got shot in the back and died. They had two witnesses that say they saw me do it."

"Where were you during the murder?" Tap asked.

"I was so mad at him that I went to the office and drank myself to sleep. They arrested me asleep in my own chair. Not one bullet missing from my gun or my bullet belt, but they claimed I pumped four shots into old Billingsly."

"So what happens next?"

"I'm scheduled to be hung within the week."

"You got any ideas who could have done it?"

"Nope. But those witnesses know it wasn't me."

"Who were they?"

"Looked like a couple of drifters."

"You got any names?"

"One was called Jacob Rippler, and the other was . . . well, his name was Three Fingers Slim."

"He ought to be easy to find."

"I would guess they got paid off and are long gone by now. But they claimed not to know each other. One was just standing around by himself on the north side of the street, and the other happened to be on the south side. They repeated the exact same story."

"No one sees a shootin' exactly like the other guy."

"I pointed that out to the judge, but it didn't seem to hold much authority. I won a race horse from that judge last spring, and I don't figure he's ever forgiven me."

"So what can I do?"

"I've got some papers you can take to the governor's office. If approved, it means he'll review my case, and that will postpone any hanging for a while."

"You want me to walk into the governor's office?" Tap asked.

"It's no big deal. You aren't wanted in Colorado, are you?"

"I don't think so."

"Well, just give the papers to a man named Whitney. He'll give you a signed receipt, and that might buy me some time."

"Then I'll try to track down those drifters."

"If they don't haul me out and lynch me first."

"Who would want to do that?"

"Billingsly's bunch. And the one who really did the killin'."

"How am I going to get the papers? The deputy said I couldn't take anything from you. Is that legal for him to say that?"

"Nope, but I don't want him to know what I'm doin' anyway. When he walks up here, lean against the bars with the back of that store-bought coat, and I'll slip them in your pocket."

"Okay. Wade, I'll do my best for you."

"I know it, Tap. I've been in Denver close to five years, and I don't trust a one of the other lawyers in town. That's why I sent for you. I heard through the boys that a mean brown-eyed, gunslingin' ladies' man from Arizona by the name of Tap was out on the North Platte. But be careful. Whoever is tryin' to set me up is not above shootin' a man in the back."

"What do you mean you sent for me?"

"You didn't get a message from me? I sent it with the stage driver to McCurley Hotel."

"When?"

"A week, ten days ago. I didn't want to pull you into this, but you're the one man I knew who wouldn't back down from a fight and couldn't be bought. But if you didn't come because of my message, why did you come?"

"Now listen, Wade, I don't want no guffaw from you, but I aim to get married . . . and—"

"What? Who are you kiddin'? Tap Andrews married?" Wade hollered.

"Hush! Let me finish."

"You find some rich widow? Shoot, they didn't even need to be widows, right?"

"Would you settle down, or I'll haul you out and lynch you myself. It's a long story that I'll tell you after I get you out of here and you come visit my ranch."

"You got a ranch?"

"Sort of. Now listen to me . . . I need to get out of a squeeze down in Arizona myself. I don't want to get married and spend the next thirty years dodging bounty hunters and lawmen. I need a lawyer to go to work for me."

"Doesn't that beat anything?" Wade laughed. "You showed up at the right time even though you didn't get my message. That's sort of providential . . . if a man believed in that sort of thing."

"I do."

Wade stared at Tap for a moment. "I've got to meet this lady of yours," he crowed. "She's got you hogtied and whipped into shape. You might amount to something yet, boy. It's a long way from those old days along the Pecos."

"We both might amount to somethin' if we can keep from gettin' hung," Andrews added.

"Time's up down there," the jailer called as he walked toward Wade Eagleman's cell. Tap turned to face the jailer but leaned against the bars.

"Get your coat away from that cell, mister," the jailer called.

"Sorry!" Tap replied. "I'm not too used to this new suit."

"Everyone can see that," the jailer growled.

"Well, I'll try to visit with you again, Mr. Eagleman. *Voy a ver al gobernador, compadre.*"

"You two Mexicans speak English, you hear me?" the jailer snapped.

Tap stared the jailer in the eyes. "Mister, if you're trying to insult me, you'll have to find a better term than that."

As he walked out of the jail, Tap heard the deputy ask Eagleman, "Who was that guy?"

"It was Billy the Kid," Eagleman teased.

"Billy was killed down in New Mexico last year," the guard reminded him.

"*Si, señor*, but that was hees ghost!" Eagleman answered.

Tap laughed all the way to the governor's office.

3

Long evening shadows lapped the streets of Denver like a silent winter plague by the time Tap arrived at the Colorado governor's office. The governor's secretary, Mr. Whitney, agreed to review the papers Wade Eagleman had sent. Hurrying back through the chill of the evening, Tap returned to the hotel and changed back into his duckings. He strapped on his Colt, buttoned the top button of his brown coat, and yanked down his hat. He picked up his Winchester '73 and then set the rifle back down in the corner of the room, leaning it against the faded green ivy on the wallpaper. He glanced in the small broken mirror beside the hotel door and brushed some road dust from his coat.

Well, Andrews, at least now you look human. The Lord never intended man to wear a store-bought suit and tie. That's why He dressed Adam and Eve in hides! God makes the bugs that live under rocks, so I guess he can create folks who like city life . . . but you surely aren't one of 'em.

He felt crowded in and yet alone as he walked down the streets of Denver. People were bundled up and looking down at their feet as they hurried to somewhere. Even the children had lost their natural smiles to the cold. His burgundy silk bandanna felt cold as it rubbed back and forth on his neck.

Tap entered the Plainsman Cafe & Saloon just as the sun dropped below the snow-capped peaks in the west. He asked the overweight bartender if he knew anything about Jacob Rippler or a man called Three Fingers Slim.

"Never heard of 'em," the man everyone called Tubby replied.

After the Plainsman came the Ponderosa Club, the Johnson Hotel, The Palomino, Evangeline's Card Room & Dance Hall, the Central Hotel, George W. Sampson's Fine Drinking Emporium, Butch's Water Hole, the Aurora Club, Cactus Curley's, the Lone Star Saloon, the Vicksburg Cafe, and Samantha's Place.

It was after 3:00 A.M. when Tap finally returned to his hotel room. While none of the bartenders, card sharks, soiled doves, or hangers-on knew Rippler, almost all of them knew someone named Three Fingers.

Three Fingers Blackie.

Three Fingers Doc.

Three Fingers Abraham.

Three Fingers Dakota.

Three Fingers Henry Hardisty.

The way they talked, every other man in Denver had only three fingers.

Look . . . it's me, Tap Andrews. You know, it's as if everything I do is a side trail away from the main road. I just want to marry Pepper and settle down. But along the way, I got to reconcile this thing in Arizona. Which led me to try and get Wade out of jail. Now I've got to find these men. You know, Lord, I'd sort of like to head back to the main trail pretty soon. If there's somethin' You'd like to do to help, well, it surely would be appreciated.

He slid the brass bed away from the window and against the east wall. He checked the chambers of his Colt. Finding five beans in the wheel, he tossed the gun next to the pillow. Then he positioned the Winchester close by the bed on the floor, pointing at the doorway. Leaving his boots and ducking trousers also next to the bed, he turned the lantern off and crawled under the clean sheets in his long-handled underwear.

A heavy rap on his door caused him to sit straight up and grab his .44 revolver. The noise continued as he fumbled his way out of the four-poster brass bed and stumbled across the unfamiliar dark hotel room. He pulled on his trousers as he hobbled.

"Yeah?" Tap finally called.

"You the fella lookin' for a three-fingered man?"

"Yep. Three Fingers Slim."

Tap scooted over to the wall on the left side of the doorway, his revolver in his right hand.

"We've got a message for you."

We? How many are there?

Tap fought back the sleep in his mind and tried to think clearly.

"Go ahead. I'm listenin'."

"No. It's a written note. Open the door. We've got orders to hand it to you personally."

"Orders from who?"

"The boss. Now come on and open up. Then we can go back and report that you got the note."

You woke me up in the middle of the night to hand me a written note? You think I've been livin' in a cave with the bears?

His eyes adjusted to the dim light as he held the revolver straight in front of his face, the barrel pointed to the ceiling, the hammer cocked.

"Slip it under the door."

"How do we know you're really the man we're lookin' fer?"

"Come back and see me in the mornin'," Tap called. "I'm goin' back to bed."

"Wait . . . here. Here's the . . . eh, note!"

He watched a white piece of paper being shoved halfway under the door. Then it stopped.

Oh, sure, push it halfway under. Do they think I'm going to fall for this?

Taking a long boot hook off the dresser, Tap used it to slide the note on into the room. The second the note began to move, four rapid gunshots splintered the door and slammed into the floor of the room. Tap crouched beside a dresser waiting for someone to burst through.

Instead he heard boot heels crashing back down the hall. Tap fumbled with the key. The lock was jammed. It was his boot heel that opened the battered door. Cautiously, he stepped out into the darkened hall. He continued down the stairs barefoot into the deserted lobby and out the front door.

The cold night air slapped his face and sent shivers down his back. His toes began to cramp on the frigid sidewalk. Tap couldn't tell which way the men had run. Returning to the lobby of the hotel, he met the night manager.

"Mr. Andrews, was there shooting in your room?"

"Yep."

"Did anyone get shot?"

"Nope."

"Oh, thank heaven. You know, blood stains are so arduous to remove."

"I've never given it much thought."

"Well, Mr. Andrews, I'm afraid I'll have to ask you to leave the hotel."

"What?"

"The discharge of firearms within the hotel is against our rules, and you will be required to seek other accommodations."

"Look, mister, I didn't fire a weapon. Someone shot at me! You can kick those other old boys out of the hotel, providin' you can run them down. And give me a room that doesn't have the front door shot out."

"Well! I'm afraid you don't understand. I can't just—"

"Mister, I'm sleepy, freezin', and too tired to talk to you. Give me a key for a fresh—"

"I most certainly will not! You must think I can be intimidated by your . . ."

Tap cocked the hammer on the Colt and pointed it up at the expensive cut-crystal chandelier hanging above the lobby.

"No!" the man called out. "Wait . . . You can have another room. But only until tomorrow."

Tap took the key from the trembling man's hand.

"And this time, don't give my room number out to other people. I'd like to get a little sleep."

By the time he had moved his belongings to the new room, he could tell that morning was just about to break out on the eastern plains. He figured on sleeping a couple hours.

He slept until almost noon.

"Mr. Andrews!" a man called at the door.

Tap quit tugging on his tall stovepipe black boots and reached for his Colt. "Yeah?"

"This is the hotel manager. I presume you will want to check out now. I believe the night manager explained that to you."

Tap sat on the edge of the bed. "Let me get this straight. He gave out my name to men who tried to kill me, and I have to leave? Perhaps I should warn the other guests of your willful disregard for the health and safety of those who stay here."

There was silence at the door.

"Eh . . . does this mean you'd like to stay another day?"

"I just might stay a month," Tap informed the man.

"Yes . . . well . . . I'll sign you in for tonight."

"Much obliged."

Within a few minutes, Tap was standing out on the wooden sidewalk in front of the Drovers' Hotel, his rifle draped over his shoulder. He waited for several wagons to roll past, and then he crossed the street.

He finished a large chop of fried rare beef at The Palomino and was staring at a hairline crack in the blue porcelain coffee cup he was holding when a short man with a long, dark gray wool topcoat stopped at his table.

"Say, ain't you the one looking for Three Fingers Slim?"

Tap glanced the man over and answered, "Yeah."

"Well, I work here at The Palomino. Last night I overhead you askin' around. Yes, sir, when I ran across those boys, I sent them right over to the Drovers' Hotel to look for you."

Tap swallowed the last of the lukewarm, bitter coffee. "Who did you send over?"

"Three Fingers Slim and that other fella. Yes, sir, I found them for you."

"You sent them to see me at four in the morning?"

"Oh, well, I'm not sure what time it was. Did they find you all right?"

"Yeah . . . they found me."

"Good. Good. I was hoping it would all work out. I could tell you really wanted to find them. Say . . . would you say a favor like that would be worth a couple dollars?" the man asked. "I lost a little at the poker table after work and find myself short this mornin'. I heard you might be willin' to pay for findin' your friends."

"You want to get paid for sending those snakes to my hotel door?"

"I certainly didn't have to do it. It was only out of my generous nature that I sent them along. I just figured it would be worth something to you."

"Well, I certainly want to give you what it's worth," Tap muttered.

"Thank you. Thank you very much."

"But it's illegal to discharge a firearm inside the cafe. So I guess I'll just pistol-whip you." Tap stood up rapidly with his Colt in his right hand.

"You'll do what?" the man gasped.

"You sent two men to my room who pumped four bullets through the door tryin' to kill me. Now tell me why I owe you some money."

"They tried to shoot you?" the man gasped. "But . . . but . . . I thought they were your associates. They said they were friends of yours."

"Friends? I don't even know them—never seen them in my life! I still don't know what they look like." Tap continued to hold the gun on the man, and some of the restaurant patrons moved back away from their tables.

"You don't mean they actually tried to kill you?"

"That's what I said. And I don't know where to find them to pay back my respects."

"Well, that won't exactly be a problem. I just saw them ride out of town to the west toward the mountains on a mule and a roan not more than thirty minutes ago."

Tap pushed himself away from the table and retrieved his rifle that had been stashed by his chair.

"Are you goin' to go out to kill 'em?" the wide-eyed man queried.

Tap left fifty cents on the table for the meal and started toward the door. "Shoot them? Shoot them?" He scowled. "Do I look like the kind of man who would provoke a gunfight?"

"Well, eh . . . actually, yeah . . . but I didn't mean nothin'. Don't take no offense," the man stammered, shifting from one foot to the next.

"I don't think I'll shoot them. Maybe just hang them instead," Tap added.

After he turned toward the door, a wide smile broke across his face.

It took him less than twenty minutes to get to the livery, saddle Brownie, and make it to the main road leading west out of Denver. The days were getting short, and the bright, cold, yellow sun was halfway along its downward descent toward the front range of the Rocky Mountains. The blue sky looked as frigid as the wind felt.

For seven miles he argued with himself.

Andrews, you don't know what these men look like; you don't know for sure this is the road they took, and you don't even know that man in the cafe was tellin' you the truth. Maybe the whole thing's just a stretcher to get you out of town. Maybe it's a setup, and they'll ambush you along the way. Or maybe that old boy doesn't know a buffalo chip from a custard pie.

He ran Brownie at a trot, trying to gain time, until he reached the Seven Mile Saloon. A mule and a roan were tied off to a leafless cottonwood tree by the back door. The hitching rail in front sported a dozen horses. He tied Brownie to the front rail and eased his way into the stuffy, smoky saloon.

Card games flourished along the south wall. On the north was a fifty-foot-long polished oak bar with a huge mirror. A crude oil painting of Jenny Lind supervised the whole saloon. Both the card tables and the bar were packed.

Stepping to the rear of the building, he huddled near the potbellied wood stove to warm his hands. Two gray-whiskered men sat on the floor with their backs to the wall near the stove, sound asleep.

Three Fingers and Rippler are probably those two on the end of the bar. They look like they're ready to bolt out the back door if anyone presses them.

Tap had never seen the two before. He was hoping they didn't recognize him either. He waited until he could confirm that the tall, thin one had only three fingers on his right hand. Then he walked over to the bar and scooted up next to the shorter of the two. He felt their gaze, but he could tell that they didn't recognize him.

"Say," Tap began, "are you boys headin' into Denver? I'm goin' in, but I don't know my way around much."

"Nope," the short one answered downing a rye whiskey.

"Do you know anything about Denver? I'm lookin' for some men, and I don't know where to find them."

"Who you lookin' for?" the tall one asked.

"The Lane brothers. You ever heard of them? One's called Jim-One and another Jim-Two. Say, you aren't the Lane brothers . . . are you?"

"I heard they're dead," the thin one answered. A faint smile broke across his unshaven face. "Most folks call me Three Fingers Slim."

"I'm Jacob," the taller one added. "And yourself?"

Tap leaned forward and whispered, "Boys . . . I think it would be safer for you two if you didn't know my name, *comprende?*"

"Why? You got a reward on your head?"

Tap glanced around the room full of men, each one looking trail-worn, each sporting a six-gun on the hip. Still whispering, Tap replied, "Let's just say there are men in this room who would try to shoot me on sight if they heard my name."

Both men looked Tap up and down.

"How do you know we won't shoot you?" the one named Jacob asked.

"'Cause you boys look a little smarter than the others. You don't seem like the type that would draw cold on a man you never seen handle a revolver. Can I buy you a drink?"

"Ain't never refused a free drink." Slim shook his head eagerly.

The bartender set up two more rye whiskeys, and Tap tossed him a coin but declined a drink himself.

"Anyway," Tap continued, "I need to find a couple of boys to throw in with me on a job down in Arizona. Now if you could tell me where those on the dodge hang out in Denver—especially the shootin' type . . . well, I'd be much obliged."

"What kind of job you got down there?" Three Fingers Slim asked.

Again Tap whispered, "I'm sorry, boys, I'm just not at liberty to say. You know—in a crowded bar like this."

"You talkin' about a payin' job, mister?"

"It's even bigger than money. Did you boys ever hear of Pat Garrett?"

"Shoot, ever'body knows he gunned down Billy the Kid," Jacob said, wiping his mouth on his dirty brown coat sleeve.

"Well . . . when I finish this job, I'll be more famous than Pat Garrett. Now I've said too much already. Too bad you boys aren't headed into Denver. We could discuss it on the trail."

"If this job's in Arizona, why are you ridin' into Denver, mister? You could probably find some men in this room who could do the job."

Tap lifted his hat and brushed back his dark brown hair. "I'm just goin' to Denver to gather a couple of sure guns to ride with me. This is not a time to hire amateurs, if you catch my drift."

"Well, now . . . we ain't goin' back to Denver, right, Slim?" Jacob put in. "We sort of . . . you know, finished a job and need to stay out of town for a while."

"You know, Jake, a little desert air might be just the ticket for us. It could be, mister, we might be the very boys you need. Now what is this all-important job?"

"I do appreciate the offer, but to tell you the truth, I'm goin' to need top hands here. Is there any truth in the rumor that John Wesley Hardin escaped from prison?"

"I ain't heard nothin' about that." Slim rubbed his tobacco-stained, wispy beard.

"Well, I'd like to bring you along, but I've got to have some men who can look down the barrel of a .44 without battin' an eye."

"Are you sayin' we can't pull our freight in a gunfight?"

Andrews looked around the crowded bar. *I've got to get them away from this crowd!* "Can we talk about this out back?" he suggested.

"That table over by the stove is private enough. Besides, these are all friends of ours anyway." Slim led the way to the table carrying a bottle and a couple of glasses. He plopped down with his back to the wall.

Andrews, if you don't get them out on the trail, you have to leave them in this saloon.

Jacob spoke first. "Now, mister, what's all this secret stuff about?"

"Well, boys, listen up." Tap's eyes searched the room, as if insuring that no one was listening. "I've been hired to do a job down in the A. T. Now I'll need—"

"What kind of job?" Slim asked.

"I'm gettin' to that. Just hold on. I'm goin' to hijack a payroll wagon headin' up to Jerome and—"

"It better be an awful big payroll for all the buildup you been givin' it!"

"If you boys interrupt me one more time, I'm ridin' down the trail," Tap insisted. "Now you got enough sense to shut up and listen, or do I ride?"

"Ain't nobody going to talk to me that way," Jacob huffed and reached for his holster.

With one motion Tap grabbed Rippler's right wrist with his left hand and pulled his own Colt with his right. The effect—Tap had his revolver cocked and jammed into the man's stomach before either could say another word.

"Wait a minute, mister," Slim interceded. "Wait . . . He didn't mean nothin'. Did you, Jake?"

"No, sir. No, sir! I surely didn't mean to rile ya."

One of the bartenders stepped over carrying a short-barreled shotgun. "You got any trouble over here, Jake?"

"Nah," Tap replied. "I was just showin' them a new move with my .44. Right, boys?"

"Yeah," Slim added. "It was pretty slick too."

The bartender retreated to work. The noise of the room rose louder and louder.

"Okay, now I'll finish." Tap reholstered his Colt. He noticed that Jacob Rippler had broken out in a sweat. "The holdup is just a cover. Oh, the take could be fifteen or twenty thousand. Me and the others will get to split that, but in the process we are suppose to make sure the man riding guard is killed."

"So someone wants to do away with a guard, and they hired you to make it look like just a holdup?" Slim asked.

"Now you got it."

"Well, I still don't see how you can compare that with Pat Garrett."

"What you didn't ask me, boys, is who the guard is."

"Well, who is he?"

"Stuart Brannon."

"You're joshin' now, right?" Slim asked.

"I heard he died down in Mexico," Rippler put in.

"I guarantee that he's still alive."

"Three or four men can't bring down Brannon. Ain't you never read none of them books?"

"If I can find the right men, we can. The one who hired me knows the exact wagon route. Can you imagine what the history books will say about those who outsmarted Brannon, the Arizona legend?"

"What's your plan?"

"I can't tell you the details now. Anyway, what I'm goin' to need is a couple of convincing decoys and another sure hand with a Colt."

"That's all it will take?"

"I see no reason to further divide either the riches or the glory. Do you?"

"We get paid up front?"

"Well, the men I hire will get one hundred dollars cash when we first start out to Arizona and then split the take even up when the job's done."

"That ain't all that much to go up against Brannon."

"Can you imagine what the history books will say about the ones who do it? Boys, we will be livin' legends in our own time!"

"Well, we *are* gettin' a little low on funds." Slim glanced over at Jacob Rippler. "What do you think?"

"Maybe the desert air would do us good," the man conceded.

"Now there's just one thing. I can't go around hirin' men I'm not sure of. What have you boys been up to lately? Who you been runnin' with?" Tap poured each of them another drink from Slim's bottle.

"Listen, mister, you ain't dealin' with no amateurs here. That old boy at the Drovers' Hotel learned that in a hurry this mornin'. Right, Jacob?"

Tap's hand slipped down the walnut grip of his Colt. Then he relaxed and brought it back above the table.

"Oh?"

"You see, this cowboy came nosin' around about another job we did, so we done him in. That's the way we operate," Jacob boasted.

Three Fingers Slim glanced at his partner. "I'll tell you who we been workin' with."

Jacob cautioned, "Maybe you shouldn't, Slim. I mean, we told him we wouldn't mention—"

"This is different. He needs to know jist what kind of hombres he's dealin' with," Slim insisted. "We was workin' with none other than Vic Barranca!"

Barranca? So he is in the area. I should have known it would be some back-shooter like Barranca.

"Victor? My old *compadre* Victor is around? Now this is a streak of luck. He's just the man I need to hold the other gun. I thought Victor got chased all the way back to the Indian Nation."

"Well, he's back now. We ought to know. We just pulled a job with him in Denver that paid us quite handsome."

"He's not in jail, is he?" Tap asked.

"Nope. And here's the good part. We done it so slick that they've done arrested and convicted another fella."

"Some firecracker Injun lawyer is goin' to hang, and it was old Barranca that put a bullet in the fella. It's almost too good to be true, ain't it?"

"Well, let's go see Barranca. He'll surely be surprised to see me."

"Eh . . . 'fraid we cain't do that." Slim shrugged. "We ain't real popular in Denver right now."

"You mean Victor's still in Denver?"

"Yep, but he's livin' on the sly, if you know what I mean. They don't know he done it, but he ain't takin' no chances."

Tap blew his breath into his hands and rubbed them back and forth. "Listen, I've got an idea. Let's sneak into town, get Victor to join us, and ride south. When we get to Colorado Springs, you'll have that one hundred dollars in hand."

"You got that money on you right now?"

"Of course not. That's another reason I need to go into Denver. You boys aren't tryin' to arrange an ambush, are you?"

"Well, we ain't goin' into Denver. Barranca said our lives would be in extreme danger if we hung around too long. Right, Jacob? So we jist might stay right here and drink 'til spring."

"Or until our funds run out. Besides, how can you be so sure Barranca will join you? He ain't the kind who takes orders from nobody."

"What? You think he'd pass up a chance to lead down Brannon? Victor and me have been shootin' our way across the West for years."

Mostly at each other, of course.

"I'll tell you what." Tap reached into his jacket and pulled out some coins. "You take this ten dollars as a down payment and wait right here. I'll be back in a day with Barranca and your one hundred dollars. Then we'll ride south and do that job. Now where do I find Barranca?" He dropped the coins into Slim's hand.

"I don't know that we should tell ya, mister. Victor would shoot us down at first sight if he know'd we told anybody where he was stayin'. He's touchy that way, don't ya know?"

"Of course, I won't tell him how I found him." Tap reached over and snatched the coins. "But I think maybe I've been wastin' my time, boys. The deal's off. I've been sittin' in this smoky saloon too long. You go on back to your drinkin'. I'm headin' into the history books." He stood up and started to walk toward the front door of the Seven Mile Saloon.

"Wait a minute, mister! Now jist don't go off gettin' your egg fried. You bein' a friend of Barranca's, I don't suppose it would hurt." Slim looked back at Jacob who nodded agreement. Slim continued, "Do you know where the Pearly Gate Dance Hall is?"

"I can find it."

"Well, you go into the Pearly Gate and ask for Lena. Tell her that Earp and Holiday sent you in to talk to Barranca. Maybe she'll take you to him . . . and maybe she won't. Now how about them coins?"

"Earp and Holiday?"

"Secret passwords."

Clowns . . . the West is filling up with idiots and clowns!

Tap tossed the coins back into the man's outstretched hands.

"I'll see you boys right here by noon tomorrow."

Tap walked out to the rail and cinched the saddle tight on Brownie. The sun had dropped behind the Rockies as he rode back into Denver. The cold, slick saddle leather sapped the heat out of his legs; the ducking trousers felt stiff and raw. He considered tying his bandanna around his almost numb ears, but ruled it out and yanked down his wide-brimmed gray hat instead.

Tap let the reins drop around the saddle horn and stuffed both gloved hands into his coat pockets to try to keep them warm. An occasional touch with a spur or a correction with a knee was all Brownie needed to keep plodding back to town. The bull-hide boots crammed into the tapaderas kept some warmth in his feet.

Barranca! Lord, the last time we went head to head I swore I'd shoot him on sight if I ever spotted him again. But even if he is the one who killed Crawford Billingsly, I've got no way to prove it. And he's not goin' to walk into the marshal's office and turn himself in.

It was well after dark when he left Brownie at the Wyoming

Stables again and returned to the Drovers' Hotel. The night clerk refused to look at him as he crossed the lobby. After washing up in a basin in his room, he went down to the hotel restaurant. He was drinking hot coffee and chewing on a tough piece of venison when the waiter, a man by the name of Maurice, scooted a chair up to his table.

"Did you want to talk to me?" he asked.

Tap swallowed a lump of gristle and looked at the man. "You ever heard of the Pearly Gate Dance Hall?"

Maurice silently looked Tap up and down.

"Listen, mister, if you are just lookin' for a girlfriend for the night, well, there's a lot safer places than the Pearly Gate. It's one of those snake holes that seems to have a knifin' or a shootin' most ever' night."

"It sounds mighty exciting. Think I'll give it a try. Where did you say it was?"

"Go up here two blocks and turn right. Then go out that diagonal road to the southeast 'til you think you're clear out of town. You'll see it on the rise. Where do you want your belongings sent when they bring you back stretched out on a board?"

Tap stared at the man for a moment. Maurice broke into a knowing smile.

"It can't be all that bad," Tap commented.

"Oh, it can be much worse. But you'll survive. I heard about the shootin' up in your room last night. Isn't your first trip to town, is it?"

"Nope."

"It will be crowded tonight."

"I'm goin' to wait and go tomorrow."

"It will be crowded then too. Every rough character on the plains heads there to get . . . eh, warm."

"Well, I don't aim to dance. I just need to ask a few questions."

"I doubt there's anyone in the place that would give you an honest answer to any question," Maurice informed him.

"That's why I'll wait until tomorrow night. I'm still half froze. Besides, I don't have any idea what kind of questions I need to ask."

After moving the brass bed again, locking the door, and placing his firearms nearby, Tap turned off the lamp and crawled under a stack of quilts.

It took him close to an hour to finally get warm.

It was even longer than that before he could get to sleep.

Now, Lord, this is Tap, and to tell You the truth, things are gettin' real confusin'. I mean, out at the ranch everything looks clear and simple. But here . . . Well, it's different. If I find Barranca, there'll be a shootin'. If I kill him, there won't be any way to prove that he's the one that back-shot Billingsly. So that means Wade's still goin' to be hung, and I'm on the run out of Colorado.

Shoot, maybe I'll just tell Wade there's nothin' I can do and ride back to the ranch. Maybe Pepper's right, Lord. The past is too messed up to try and straighten out. Maybe there's a time to just walk away from it.

Tap rolled over in the dark room and let his hand drop to the floor. He could feel his Winchester. And his boots.

Lord, You know I can't do that. You been houndin' me about Arizona. And now I can't leave Wade in jail. He might not be a deacon in the church, but he's my friend, and he's been dealt a crooked hand. Help me figure this one out.

What little sleep Tap could grab ended when the first ray of daylight filtered through the thin curtains of the barren room at the Drovers'.

Within minutes he had dressed, grabbed his guns, and banged his boot heels down the hall. A blurry-eyed Maurice met him in the parlor.

"Are you comin' in or goin' out?" he asked.

Tap sighed and lifted his rifle from his shoulder. "I'm goin' out, Maurice."

"Nothin' in town open yet but the all-night saloons."

"I'm headin' down to the jail to visit a friend."

"You comin' back tonight?"

"Yep."

"Well, if I were you, I'd stay away from the Pearly Gate. It's plumb cultus, if I do say so."

Tap broke into a wide grin. "You know, Maurice, you've warned me about that place so often I've just got to check it out. Couldn't be any place north of Hades with that bad a reputation."

"Who said it was north of Hades?"

Tap didn't bother wearing the store-bought suit this time. He entered the jail and asked a startled jailer if he could visit with Wade Eagleman.

"At this time in the mornin'? Nobody allowed in until after 10:00 A.M. Mister, I ain't even fed the prisoners breakfast. Is it daylight out there?"

"It's fast gettin' that way."

"Well, I guess you can wait out here. It's better you came to see him today than a couple days from now."

"How's that?" Tap asked.

"Well, you know . . . the hangin's goin' to be the day after tomorrow."

"Hangin'? I thought the governor was reviewing the case."

"Don't know nothin' about that. But he'll be hanging soon, that's for sure. I'll come get you when it's visitin' time."

"I'll go to the livery and take care of my horse. Are you sure I can't get in until 10:00?"

"Yep."

Tap groomed Brownie, ate breakfast, and paced in front of the jail. Finally the jailer appeared at the door and signaled him in.

"Just remember—"

"Keep my hands away from the bars."

"And you can lay those weapons of yours right here on the table."

Tap did so and then sauntered down the stark corridor and stopped by Wade Eagleman's cell.

"Tap! You look human. Thanks for not wearin' those store boughts."

"You haven't been sittin' in there bein' jealous of my fine vest, have you?"

"What else do I have to think about? After all, I've got forty-eight hours before they hang me. What happened to those papers?"

"I gave them to Mr. Whitney at the governor's office. He said he'd review the case. I told them this had to be taken care of immediately."

"Well, if they take a couple more days, it won't matter," Wade muttered.

"I'll head right over to the governor's office and see what happened." Then Tap lowered his voice. "I know who shot Billingsly."

"Who?"

"Barranca."

"Vic Barranca? But isn't he serving time in Texas? Or was it New Mexico?"

"Both. But he's here in town, and your driftin' accusers said it was Barranca."

"You found them?"

"Yeah. But I couldn't talk them out of their rat hole."

"It doesn't look good, Tap. I've got too much Indian blood. No one will give it a second thought. I've seen it go this way before."

"Maybe I can round up a crew, and we'll try to bust you out," Tap whispered.

"Right at the moment anything sounds mighty good."

"Look, I've got to go talk to that fellow Whitney and then confront Barranca. I'll be back and let you know."

"I'm not goin' anywhere."

"Wade, I'll be back or I'll be dead. You can count on it."

"I know . . . thanks. If I get out of this thing, I owe you a big one, partner."

"*When* you get out. I've got that big one already lined up!"

Tap was standing on the front steps of the governor's office when the first few staff members came back from their lunch break and let him in.

"I need to talk to either the governor or Mr. Whitney."

An older gray-haired man flashed a pleasant smile.

"Yes, well, wait right here, please."

Tap waited. And waited. And waited.

It was after 3:00 P.M. before the man returned to the hallway.

"Now you wanted an appointment with the governor?"

"Yeah, I've been waitin' all afternoon!"

"How is Thursday? At 10:30 A.M.? What is the nature of your business?"

"What! I've got to speak to the governor today!"

"I'm afraid that would be impossible."

"It's a matter of life and death and—"

"Well, sir, I'm certainly sorry for that, but the governor's left for the day."

"How about Mr. Whitney?"

"I'm afraid he's gone too."

"So who's in charge now? I brought some papers for a review of a hangin' case, and I want to make sure something gets done about it!" Tap's voice rose.

"Oh, I'm sorry. No one in the office is qualified to handle that kind of work but Mr. Whitney. And the governor, of course."

"You mean an innocent man could hang because everyone happens to be gone for the day!" Tap hollered.

"If you'll come back on Thursday at—"

"Next Thursday! Wade will be dead by then!" Tap bellowed.

"I'll have to ask you to leave!"

"You're goin' to have to ask me to do a whole lot more than . . ." Tap started to draw his Colt, then stopped himself, spun on his heels, and left the governor's office.

Lord, an innocent man's about to be hung, and nobody cares! I mean, nobody but You and me.

The Pearly Gate Dance Hall lived up to its reputation. It was just getting dark when Tap finally found the place. Several men were passed out on the front porch in the cold November air. One man came flying out the door and landed face first in the street. He rolled over and crawled to the wooden sidewalk.

The smoke and noise was so thick inside that Tap had to pause by the door and wait until he could distinguish the drunks from the dance-hall girls.

He crowded up to the bar and shoved in between a bearded old man who appeared to be asleep and a man with a wispy goatee and a bright red face.

"What are you drinkin', mister?" the bartender hollered.

"Just need to ask a question."

"If you ain't drinkin', get out of here!"

"Look, would you just tell me which gal is Lena?"

"Get out of here! The bar is for payin' customers!"

"Set me up with rye whiskey," Tap conceded.

The man came over, wiped out a used glass with his dirty apron, and filled it halfway. "That's a dollar."

"What?"

"It's a dollar! You tryin' to cause trouble?" the bartender growled.

Just as the bartender reached to pick up the coin Tap had tossed on the sticky bar, Tap reached up and grabbed the man by the shirt collar and with one motion dragged him halfway over the bar. Then he poured the drink over the man's head.

Those around him, except for the sleeping old man, pulled back and gave them room as the crowd's roar ceased.

"Now I asked which one of these gals is Lena."

A husky, yet familiar voice rolled across the crowded room. "You lookin' for me, cowboy?"

Dropping the grip on the bartender, Tap spun around and stared through the smoky haze.

"Rena?" he gasped.

"Tap?" Her painted smile froze in place. "I thought you were still at A. T. P.!"

4

The first night after Tap left for Denver, Pepper sipped coffee in the kitchen of the hotel with Mrs. McCurley until 8:00 P.M. It was a cold night, but the kitchen was warm at the verge of being too warm. To Pepper it felt like when she had one too many blankets on the bed—too comfortable to do anything about it, but just sweat a little.

Her long, curly blonde hair wouldn't stay back in the combs, and after helping serve the guests, she just let it drop down to her shoulders. She held a silver tray up like a mirror and stared into her green eyes.

Twenty-five going on forty. Girl, you're never goin' to get rid of those crow's feet around your eyes. Your nose is too small, your chin is too pointed, and your cheeks are too round. Not to mention a mouth too wide and lips too full.

A wide grin broke across her face.

Other than that, you're a real head-turner! Lord, what does Tap see in me anyway?

Pepper hung her apron on a hook near the back door. She scooted through the near empty parlor and up the stairs to her room without speaking to anyone.

For almost two months she had enjoyed the most peaceful routine in her entire life. She would ride out to the ranch to be with Tap at least once a week (and he would come see her every Sunday). Then there were occasional trips with the McCurleys to visit friends, some work at the hotel just to keep busy, and time spent reading Suzanne Cedar's Bible. Before it got so cold, she took regular long walks along the river. And there was always plenty of time for sleep. She felt as if she was being allowed to catch up on every night of missed sleep for the past ten years.

Shutting the door behind her, she turned up her lamp and closed the curtains on the twelve-foot by fifteen-foot room with a high ceiling that had been her home for several weeks.

She glanced at the mirror above her dresser as she slipped out of the long, green dress with lace collar and cuffs.

Well, old girl, no drunk men to dance with; no jealous girls to scream at; no one crying in the room next door; no knives, sneak-guns, or shattered glass; no rye-whiskey courage; no opium-house depression; no waking up feeling cheap and helpless . . .

Yep. You're goin' to make it, girl. The Lord gave you a chance to walk away from it all. And you did it!

Thank You, Jesus.

Still staring at the mirror, she saw lines of worry creep back around her eyes.

Lord, I want him back. I want him back right now. I want Tap to just burst through the door and say, "Pepper, the preacher's downstairs. Let's go get married!"

I don't know why he had to stir up this hornet's nest in Arizona. He's got to learn to just walk away from it all like I have.

Pepper could hear the storm lash against her window.

Keep him safe, Lord.

And keep him out of Arizona.

The early morning rap at the door startled her. She sat straight up in bed clutching a hunter green quilt tightly around her shoulders. With slightly cold fingers she rubbed the corners of her eyes and brushed her hair back over her shoulders.

She had planned on sleeping late and joining Mrs. McCurley in the kitchen somewhere between ten and eleven. The dark shadows still in the room told her it was much earlier than that.

Finally she offered a feeble, "Yes?"

"Pepper, dear, there are a couple of men here who would like to talk to you."

"Me?"

"Yes. They said they're old friends from Denver."

There's no one in Denver I ever want to see again. Besides Tap.

"Eh . . . I don't think . . ."

"Shall I tell them to call back this afternoon?" Mrs. McCurley called from the hall.

Whoever they are, I don't want to see them . . . Oh, Lord, not Dillard. Please, not him!

"I'll . . . need a while to make myself presentable. Tell them I'll be down shortly." She sighed.

"Take your time, dear. I'll feed them some breakfast."

Hurrying to get dressed, she thought of Carter Dillard.

It's him. I know it's him. I told him three years ago the debt was settled. I don't owe him a thing! He's got no business interfering with my life—not now, not ever.

She was still arguing with herself while she finally got most of her hair tucked up with combs and straightened her dress. Stopping at the mirror by the dresser, she noticed deep furrows forming at the corners of her eyes.

"Dillard, you have no part in my life, nor I in yours. I would ask you to never come to see me again!" *That's the way Suzanne Cedar would handle it.*

Pepper still tried to follow the model of the woman whose death had changed her life.

The old Pepper would just shove a knife in his soft stomach. Maybe I can find something in between.

Junior Pardee was leaning against the bottom rail of the stairs when she descended toward the dining room.

"Well . . . well, Miss Pepper! It is you, isn't it? I surely didn't hardly recognize you lookin' so . . . eh, refined and all."

"What do you want, Pardee? I ought to shoot you on sight, and you know it."

"Now, now. There's no need to snort at me. Why, if I remember right, the last time I saw you, you were wearing a highly revealing red velvet gown down at a dance hall with a drunken gunslinger draped all over you."

"No, the last time you saw me, the drunken gunslinger threw you out into the street on your ear for grabbin' at me. But if you're tryin' to embarrass me, Pardee," Pepper barked, "I'm way beyond that. Tell Dillard I don't want to see him now or ever. I would appreciate it if you two would leave these premises."

"You always were a fiery one! Yes, ma'am! But I think you'd better talk to Dillard. He was just gettin' around to tellin' old man McCurley about the time you were in a drunken stupor, and he had to take you off the street and nurse you back to health."

"No!" Pepper protested. "Where is he?"

"Ah . . . now that's better. Well, he stepped out to the barn to check on the horses. He reckoned it to be a more—what would you call it?—private place to talk."

Pepper went to the hall closet and removed her heaviest charcoal gray wool coat. Slipping into it, she tugged on her gloves and called out into the kitchen, "Mrs. McCurley? I'm stepping out to the barn. I'll be back in just a few minutes."

Junior Pardee took her by the arm to usher her outside. Her elbow crashed into his ribs, and he staggered back.

"Pardee, don't you ever, ever touch me again!" she hissed. "It would be the delight of my life to have a reason to gut-shoot you."

"One of these days you'll change that stubborn mind," he snarled, revealing tobacco-stained teeth.

A clear, frigid breeze blasted off the snow-dusted hills and took Pepper's breath away as she crunched across the yard toward the barn. Turning up the collar of her coat, she broke into a trot.

The McCurley barn was not much warmer, but it blocked the cold drift of wind. Through the dark shadows she could see a wide-shouldered, tall man hitching up two big horses to a black carriage.

"Dillard, I told you last time I don't ever want to see you again. I don't owe you nothin'! Do you hear me!" she raged.

The man turned toward her, and she recognized the hard look in his dark eyes. There was more gray hair at the temples than she remembered. The square face wore sharp lines. His bushy eyebrows looked as menacing as his heavy drooping mustache.

"Now, Miss Pepper Paige, is that any way to greet a man who saved your life and nurtured you back to health?"

"Whatever you did for me was paid in full at that reception for the governor, and you know it. You said you'd never ask me for another thing. Get out of here, Dillard!"

"Junior, didn't I say she'd be mighty glad to see me? Why, Pepper, it's really touching how emotional you are. My, you are attractive when you're angry. I think it's because when you're tense like that, your posture's better."

"Don't play games with me, Dillard. I'm going back into the house!"

"I don't think so." Dillard crossed his arms across his barrel chest.

Pepper spun toward the door and faced Junior Pardee's drawn .45. "You do remember that I ain't above shootin' women, don't ya?" Pardee growled.

"Oh, yeah. I remember you shootin' that little Celestial girl at that Denver saloon just because she said you smelled like a skunk!"

"There ain't no Chinese goin' to call me a skunk!"

"Now, Pepper, just settle down for a minute," Dillard urged. "Let me tell you what it is I need. It's not as if I'm demanding something you aren't accustomed to givin'."

She spun around and faced the black-haired man. "Make it quick, Dillard. I'm cold."

"You know you can call me Carter," he added.

"The only thing I want to call you is gone."

"Pardee, didn't I tell you Pepper would never change? Same old firecracker. You know, that's why she can still make it in the dance-hall-girl business. Most just wear themselves out at her age. Not Pepper. Now if you'll just listen a moment. I need you to do me a little favor. And I'm goin' to pay you handsome for it. I've got an important meeting with the governor. He'll be makin' some recommendations about who should get the contract to run a new rail line up from New Mexico, and I intend to get the nod."

"You don't know any more about railroads than you do gold mines!" she interjected.

"That's what I been tellin' him." Pardee scratched the back of his head with the barrel of his revolver.

"But," Dillard roared, "I know plenty about spending big money! I'll contract out all the work. I just get the profits."

"I thought the governor was a drinkin' buddy with Billingsly and that gang. They're buildin' all the railroads in Colorado. You ain't got a chance in—"

"Billingsly's dead, poor soul." Dillard laughed in a way that made the hair on the back of Pepper's neck tingle. "I'd say my upstandin' reputation puts me right in line for the contract."

"Upstandin'?" Pepper's voice rose. "You're a lyin', cheatin', murderin'—"

"No reason to recite his virtues, Miss Pepper." Pardee moved closer to Pepper from behind.

"Now sit down on that stool and shut up, and I'll tell you what I need you to do," Dillard commanded. "You're going to ride up to Hot Springs with me today. Tomorrow the governor and some other state officials are having a big party. I'll need you to attend as my wife, like you did back then. You will charm the men and make the ladies jealous and dance with the governor.

"After a couple days of negotiations, I'll land the contract, and Pardee will drive you back here to McCurley's. We'll be gone three or four days at the most. You'll end up with a couple of fine dresses and one hundred dollars cash money. I'm talkin' about a business deal that will benefit all of us."

Pepper had refused to sit down. "There's no way I'm goin' to do that. I posed as your wife once, and what did it get me? You ended up dumping me in that little cabin with six drunken drifters. If Stack hadn't rumbled along, I'd be dead now . . . or worse."

"I remember that my instructions were for them to take you promptly to April Hastings's."

"Well, they didn't remember your instructions. Forget it, Dillard. You can go buy off someone else to pretend like you're a decent man."

Pardee stepped up close to her. She smelled his whiskey breath and stepped away, which meant being closer to Dillard. "He cain't do that, Miss Pepper. Seems the governor still remembers you and asked specifically if you'd be comin' along."

"What?"

Dillard closed in, almost pinning Pepper between them. "Yes. The governor likes your dancing and asked for the privilege of a spin around the floor with the yellow-haired Mrs. Dillard."

"Look, I told you, I'm not pretendin' to be your wife—not now, not ever again. I happen to be engaged to a very fine Christian man who's a rancher in these parts. And, I might add, who will be along any time now. I do not work in a dance hall, and I do not sell my services. Now I'm goin' back into the—"

As she spun to face Pardee, Dillard grabbed her left arm and squeezed it with a viselike grip, yanking her toward him.

"That hurts!"

"Not near as much as what will happen if you refuse to come along."

Pepper kicked wildly at Dillard and missed. He grabbed her waist and lifted her straight off the ground. Then he tossed her over on a pile of straw near the carriage.

"Now you listen, and you listen careful because I don't intend on repeating this. You are goin' to go with me for four days, and you are goin' to pretend to be my wife, and you're goin' to be pleasant, and you're goin' to dance with the governor and anyone else I say.

"And I'll tell you why you're goin' to do it. Because three years ago you were eight months pregnant and smoking so much opium you couldn't crawl out of the middle of 16th Street."

"I wasn't on opium, and you know it!" she protested.

"You were so far gone you didn't know who you were, where you were, or what you were on. I hauled you out of there and put you in a room with clean sheets and warm blankets. I was the one who paid for the doctor's visits. And when the baby came early and stillborn, I was the one who saw it had a burial. I kept you out of jail and out of the newspapers. And I was the one who paid the bills when you got sick and almost died after that."

Pepper crawled to her feet and stomped over to Dillard. "I paid you off in full," she cried. "I lied for you to the governor. I helped you cheat Clifton and Frazier out of that mining claim. I stood by when you shot down Cordova. And I cleaned up your bed when you couldn't hold your liquor! And what thanks did I get? You tossed me off as a prize to the likes of Junior Pardee and gang! You . . . you . . ." Searching wildly, she grabbed up a short manure fork and waved it at the men. "Get out of here!"

Dillard stepped back and let her have some room.

Pardee moved in with his gun drawn.

"Let her go, Junior," Dillard ordered.

"What? I ain't goin' to let her go."

"She doesn't want to come with us. That's obvious."

"But—but . . . ," Junior Pardee stammered. "I don't care what you say, she ain't runnin' away from me this time. No, sir. If she ain't goin' to dance with the governor, she can dance right here with me. If you don't want her, I'll take her."

"Leave her be!" Dillard's hand dropped to the handle of his revolver.

"Who do you think—"

"I pay the salary, remember? Come on, Junior, we'll just sit here and wait for this fine Christian rancher man to come by. I think it's only fair and honest for him to know what kind of woman he's plannin' on marryin'."

"It don't matter to him," she replied, still waving the pitchfork. "He knows all about my past, and he loves me. He's goin' to marry me anyway."

"He knows everything, and he still wants to marry you? I'd say he's a little dense, ain't he?"

"He's a gunman who could cut you two down before you ever got your hog legs out of the holster."

"A gunman now? Isn't that nice? I thought he was a fine Christian man."

"He is . . ."

"Oh," Dillard said with a grin, "a fine Christian gunman. Well, I'd like to meet this man and refresh his memory on your past. Maybe there's one or two things he's forgotten."

"He's gone on a trip. He won't be back for a long time."

"I thought you said he'd be here any minute now."

"I lied."

"Well, it's good to see you haven't changed all that much. While I'm waiting for him, I think I'll go chat with the McCurleys. Nice folks, they are. Seem to think you're a respectable woman of the community. Obviously they don't know much about you either."

"Dillard . . . stay away from the McCurleys! You wouldn't do that."

"Of course I would. You just got through tellin' me how despicable I am." Dillard walked away from her toward the carriage. Then he turned back with a sly grin. "Look, Pepper, maybe I didn't treat you all that square after you recovered from the miscarriage. But all I want is four days, and then you can come back and live your life with this rancher—gunman—whoever. Do this and I won't bother you ever again. I'll be so rich I'll move off to San Francisco, and you'll be readin' about me in the newspapers. What in the world would I need to bother you about when I'm living up on the hill? Don't you see, it's the one way to get me out of your life forever. You get to have the future you want, and I'll have the future I want. Everybody's happy. I'll send you right back here in a buggy. And I'll pay you in gold."

Lord . . . this isn't fair. I can't even tell Tap about that baby. I just can't. I don't have it in me. Don't make me tell him, Lord. It's too horrible.

"What's it goin' to be, Miss Yellow Hair?" Pardee prodded. "Do you get in that carriage? Or do we go visitin' with the folks in the hotel?"

She was still staring at the carriage when Carter Dillard lifted the pitchfork out of her hand and led her over to the buggy.

"I can't go right now!" she protested. "I'll need to pack . . . and tell Mrs. McCurley."

"No need for that. I've got the dresses and everything you need to look like a rich man's wife," he countered. "Besides, your dance-hall outfits wouldn't exactly be the right thing for a high society function."

"No . . . no, I'm not that way anymore!" she protested. "Don't make me do this, Dillard. Go away. Just go away and leave me alone!"

"Darlin', a woman's past will never leave her alone. It's the life you chose to live. You reap what you sow. And now it's time to reap. It's not like it's hard work. You don't have to scrub any floors. Just wear pretty dresses, eat fancy meals, and dance with the men. Lots of gals would consider that a vacation."

"Then go get them to do it."

"I promised the governor *you* would be there."

"That's your mistake."

"No!" Dillard blew up. "My mistake was spending $200 on doctor's bills and medicine for a woman that I should have let die right out there on 16th Street! My mistake was burying a baby that only God knows who the father was. My mistake was taking you to that reception and letting you see what it's like to be considered a respectable woman. That's my mistake. Thinking I could count on a little gratitude from a dance-hall girl. Everybody told me it was a waste of money. I didn't believe them. No, I saw something more in those pretty green eyes. 'Why, she just needs a break,' I said. But maybe they were right all along. Maybe some women are destined to live life at its lowest level."

"Don't do this to me, Dillard," Pepper sobbed. "You never treated me good. You'd hit me when you were drunk and ridicule me when you was sober! I paid you back. Then you dumped me when you thought you didn't need me anymore."

"And I say you got a bargain. Maybe you've forgotten. You were too ashamed to go ask April Hastings for help. And there certainly wasn't one other man in Denver who wanted anything to do with you. You do owe me, Pepper Paige. That's why you didn't stay in your room and tell me to go away. That's why you hiked into this dark barn. That's why you haven't screamed for help. You owe me!"

Feeling dazed and disoriented, Pepper could hear herself ask, "I'll be back in four days . . . right?" It sounded like a distant voice.

"Yep."

"You won't ever look me up again?"

"Nope."

"I'll go tell Mrs. McCurley."

"Junior can tell her."

"But I've got to get my bag—my valise, some personal items."

"I'll be parked out front. If we hurry, maybe we can make Hot Springs by dark."

Pepper had her valise packed with combs, perfume, undergarments, a few personal items, and a short-nosed revolver loaded with five .32 caliber bullets. Then she wrote a hurried note that she left on her dresser. She wore her knit wool hat and carried earmuffs in her pocket.

Mrs. McCurley met her at the bottom of the stairs. "Pepper, dear, are you going on a ride?"

"An emergency has come up, and I'm afraid I'll be away for a few days. If I'm not back in four days, there's a note on my dresser. Would you please see that Mr. Andrews gets that letter as soon as possible after that?"

"Are you in danger? I can get Mr. McCurley to—"

"No. No, not yet anyway. I'll get this all cleared up and be back soon. I do hope this doesn't put you in too much of a bind in the kitchen."

"Oh, we'll manage. But do be careful. We'll miss you. Your presence puts a certain twinkle in everyone's eyes."

The carriage was rolling out of the yard and down the road to the south before Pepper's thoughts finally became clear.

"Dillard, stop the buggy! I'm goin' back. I'm not doin' this for you!" She tried to stand up in the buggy, but his strong right hand gripped the back of her neck and forced her down.

"Oh, you're goin' to do it, darlin'. You're goin' to do it for that rancher and all those little children that you want to see running around the yard someday."

"Then you keep Pardee and the others away from me!" she insisted. "I swear I'll tell the governor you're a lyin', cheatin' jerk if you don't keep him away from me."

"He won't touch you."

"And give me the buggy."

"What?"

"I want to drive a buggy back by myself."

Dillard let loose of her neck. "All right, you can have a horse and buggy."

"And a '73 carbine with ten shells."

"What do you want a carbine for?"

"To shoot Pardee and the others if they try to sneak up on me."

"You can have a carbine, but not until after you dance with the governor."

She bounced along in the buggy with a blanket over her lap for several miles without speaking. She could see frost forming on Dillard's mustache and eyebrows.

"I want my own room," she blurted out.

"What?"

"At the hotel in Hot Springs I want my own room."

"I can't go checkin' in Mr. and Mrs. Dillard and have two rooms."

"You can get one of those big suites with a sitting room. You can sleep on the settee."

"Now, Pepper, this is goin' . . ." The look in her eyes stopped him in midsentence.

"Okay, we'll have a suite."

She bounced on the buggy seat dejectedly for the next several hours. She resorted to pulling a blanket over her head and peeking out of her woolen veil only occasionally.

Lord, I shouldn't be here. I don't want to be here. I don't know how this happened, and I really don't know why it happened.

Maybe Tap's right. Some things are just goin' to follow you the rest of your life. Lord, I thought . . . You know, that . . . well . . . believin' in You and all, that those things would all be taken away.

Just this once, Lord. I'll get this settled and out of my past. Just like Tap had to take care of the Arizona matter . . . well, I have to resolve this thing with Dillard. Tap'll understand.

For a long time she rode in silence reviewing scenes from her past that she had successfully blocked out for years.

I can't admit all of that to Tap. I can't even admit it to myself.

Oh . . . Lord, that baby would be alive if I'd taken better care of myself.

I need a drink.

No, I didn't mean that. Well, I meant it . . . sort of but not really. Not any more. That's how I used to forget. But now, well, You knew about all of that from the beginning.

Just help me not do anything else I'll spend the rest of my life regretting.

By the time they rolled into Byer's Hot Sulphur Springs, it was dark, and Pepper's teeth were chattering beyond control. She took a hot bath, ate a small supper, slipped a sharp knife from the dinner table into the sleeve of her dress, and retired to the room.

When Dillard came up later, he stomped into the suite and banged on the bedroom door.

"Pepper . . . we need to talk."

"You promised to stay out there," she called.

"I'll stay out here, but we need to go over tomorrow's plans."

"We can talk about them in the mornin'."

"Don't play with me," Dillard yelled. "Open the door or I'll bust in."

"Yes, Governor," Pepper mocked, "Mr. Dillard is a swindler and a cheat, and he likes to slap women around!"

There was silence for a moment.

"Pepper, we'll have to go over what to say to the governor."

"I'll meet you in the cafe for breakfast around nine."

"Wear the green dress," he called.

Pepper didn't answer. She shut down the lamp and crawled into bed fully dressed except for her boots. The sharp knife lay within reach on a night stand. The revolver was tucked under her pillow. She hoped she wouldn't need either one during the night.

She didn't.

"Well, Mrs. Dillard, you look quite beautiful this morning."

"Save it, Dillard. There's no one in here listening to you anyway."

"You've got to call me Carter."

"I can call you a big pile of cow chips, but I'm not callin' you Carter."

"But . . . when the governor—"

"I'll call you Mr. Dillard. That's still acceptable for a woman to do."

"All right. All right. Now here's what you got to know. I've told the governor that I've been down in South America building the Quito—"

"I don't want to know," she interrupted. "Look, if I don't know anything, then I can't mess it up, nor can I be accused of lying."

"Look, you got to—"

"What I'm goin' to do is dance, smile, and tell them I know nothin' about your business ventures. That's all I said I would do. And then you're going to give me that buggy and horse, a hundred dollars in gold, and a carbine. Now that's the deal. That's all I need to know. Where's the governor?"

"Up in his room, I suppose."

"Where's Pardee and the others?"

"What others?"

"Come on, Dillard. You've got them stashed somewhere."

"There are a few men camped down from the springs."

"That's mighty nice of you letting them camp in the snow while you're in the hotel."

"They don't mind. There's hot water in the creek, and they have a keg of whiskey."

"I'm goin' back to my room," she announced.

"Just wait. The governor will be down soon."

"You can send for me."

"Relax, Pepper. We can sit here and pretend like we are enjoying each other's company. You used to do that for a living, remember?"

"I said I'd dance with the governor, but I didn't say I would sit around making small talk."

"Sit down, Pepper, before I tie you to that chair!"

"Yeah, that would look real good when the governor walked in. I said I was goin' upstairs!"

"Did someone mention me? Why, Mrs. Dillard, how lovely you look. Welcome back to the states. I presume you had as nice a time in Ecuador as Mr. Dillard."

Pepper brushed her hair back and smiled at the governor as he approached. "My days have been fairly pleasant lately. How's your back been, Mr. Governor?"

"Oh . . . Governor . . ." Carter Dillard stood and apologized, "I didn't know you had come in."

"Sit down, Carter," the governor commanded. Then he scooted a chair up next to Pepper. "Thanks for asking about my back, Mrs. Dillard. Actually, that's why I come up here to the hot springs. They seem to give me a little relief."

"My, I surely hope you'll be up to dancing tonight." She smiled.

The governor reached over and patted her right hand. "I wouldn't miss it if I were on crutches."

"Well, if you'll excuse me. I . . . eh, need a little fresh air. I thought I'd walk over to the springs."

"Certainly . . . certainly. We need to go over some boring old railroad papers anyway. Right, Carter?"

"Yes, sir. I believe you're right."

"Shall I find someone to walk with you, dear?"

"Oh, no . . . Mr. Dillard. That's not necessary." She curtsied and left the dining room.

The steam from the hot springs warmed the air on the overlook where Pepper stood. The otherwise cold morning seemed almost warm and humid. A few other people were on the promenade, and most of the women wore hats. Pepper felt self-conscious and stood off by herself.

Maybe I should go to the livery and have the boy hitch up the buggy. I could pretend to go for a ride and head back to McCurley's . . . maybe go out to the ranch and wait. By the time they found me, it would be too late for the railroad deal.

But Pardee and the others would chase me down. Maybe I could just slip out on a horse . . . or hitch a ride with someone. They could give me a lift to a stage stop. Then I could . . .

But if I destroy Dillard's big chance, he would track me down and make me pay for it. Maybe this railroad scheme is *the only way to get rid of him.*

"I beg your pardon, ma'am. Have you seen the governor?"

"What?" Pepper was startled. "Oh, the governor?"

"Yes, ma'am. I'm Mr. Whitney from Denver. I've got an important message for the governor."

"Oh my, what's happened?"

"Well, I don't think I should . . . it's just . . . well, it's just something about some murderer that's supposed to be hung."

"Oh. Well, the governor's in the back room at the cafe talking to my . . . I mean, talking to Carter Dillard."

"Thank you, ma'am."

She turned back to the steaming hot springs and searched for another escape scenario. She was still standing there when a shout startled her. It was Carter Dillard yelling from the front porch.

"Pepper! We must pack up and leave."

Lord! It all fell through! The deal's off. Dillard will have to send me back to McCurley's. But I kept my part. He should give me the buggy and horse. And the Winchester.

Dillard came running across the snow-covered yard.

"Hurry. The governor was summoned back to Denver. Something about a condemned prisoner. He's invited us to stay with him until we have the railroad matter settled! Get your things packed. This is even better than I hoped. You get to mingle with Denver's finest. Won't all the girls at April Hastings's be jealous?"

"Denver?"

"Yes, yes, but just for another day or so. The deal is just the same—"

"I'm not going to Denver!"

"Be quiet! Of course, you're going to Denver. You ride alongside me in the buggy, or I'll stuff you in a flour sack and toss you across a saddle horse, but you're going."

"Dillard, I can't go to Denver, and that's all there is to it. I won't go!"

5

Within the hour the governor's carriage rolled east from Byer's Hot Sulphur Springs toward Denver. Several coaches and wagons followed into the cold, cloudy November morning. Pepper Paige sat in the last buggy, covered by a wool blanket, a bright blue knit hat—and severe depression.

Lord, this isn't the way it was supposed to turn out. I can't go to Denver. Tap's somewhere in that town. What if he sees me with Dillard?

It would break his heart.

It would break my heart.

Please, Lord. I just want to go back and hide in Medicine Bow Mountains.

For the rest of my life.

Every bounce and jar from the rig seemed to displace her from what was happening. Pepper felt as if she were reading a very sad novel, and she was in it. Her breath fogged in front of her face as she turned to the carriage driver.

"Dillard, I told you back at the springs, I'm not going through with this. I'm goin' to catch a coach in Denver for Fort Collins. Then I'll take the stage back to McCurley's. You can tell anybody anything you want. It's just not worth it anymore. I just shouldn't be here with you. And you have no legal right to force me."

"You're getting to be a boring and tiresome woman. It will be a delight to get rid of you. But not before we go to the governor's party. So forget it. We're not ridin' around that mountain again."

There was no emotion in Dillard's voice. "Don't act like you're too good to do such a thing. I know what kind of woman you are. You owe me, and I'm collectin'."

"Don't give me that cart load of guilt. I don't need it. I pay my debts. But you have no right to ask this. Look, you sit down and figure out all the money you spent on me and the baby. Give me a statement, and I'll start tryin' to pay it off. Just tell me what I owe you. If it takes me fifty years, I'll pay you back every penny!"

"I'm afraid there's no way to calculate. Oh, there was a considerable amount of money spent. But how about all my time . . . and stress . . . and damage to my reputation? How do you figure the cost to my stature?"

"Damage to your reputation? Damage! There is no way helping me lowered that."

"Dance-hall darlin', it's not worth the effort to argue. You're going to Denver, and you're going to dance with the governor. As I see it, you either do that, or I send you home . . . with the boys."

"You promised me a carriage!"

"Only if you followed through with your promise."

"I kept my promise. I came to Hot Springs with you."

"But you haven't danced with the governor."

"You mean, I either go to Denver with you, or you'll sick Junior Pardee and the others on me?"

"Angel, I hadn't planned on using a dog analogy, but I suppose it probably fits, doesn't it?"

Pepper's tight right fist flew out of the blanket and caught Dillard hard to the bony part of his chin. He lurched back to avoid another blow and in the process jerked the reins tight, accidentally stopping the rig. Pepper's left hand came flying, and this time he dropped the reins to protect himself. He grabbed her gloved left hand before it found his half-frozen face, but she pulled back leaving him holding nothing but the glove.

Dillard's left hand clamped onto her right wrist, preventing her from landing another roundhouse. She countered by swinging the gloveless left in a slapping motion that glanced off his hand, plowing bloody furrows with her fingernails as they gouged the soft part of Dillard's neck just beneath the left side of his jaw.

Junior Pardee and four other riders galloped toward the carriage from several hundred feet behind. The noise of thundering hooves pounding the half-frozen road caused the two horses pulling Dillard's buggy to bolt off the roadway and into the snow-covered brush.

The force of the bouncing wagon jolted its passengers so violently that they fell back on the carriage seat. Dillard grabbed for the reins to gain control.

While he yelled at the horses, Pepper reached for the Colt .45 holstered at his hip, but Dillard caught her shoulder with his right hand and shoved her hard. She could feel her feet tangle in the blanket that draped her legs. She reached out wildly to clutch anything that would keep her from falling out of the runaway rig.

For a moment she held onto the wool sleeve of Dillard's heavy overcoat. But with blood trickling down his neck, he slammed the palm of his right hand against her left ear, and she tumbled out of the carriage.

Pepper heard herself scream above the roar of the carriage wheels. But the sound grew distant as she felt something hard strike her head.

Something very hard.

The little boy ran through tall summer grass that lapped above his waist. Pepper couldn't see his feet or legs—only the fresh long-sleeve, collarless cotton shirt and the brown leather suspenders. He was laughing . . . or singing a song . . . or both.

His mop of blond hair hung almost to his shoulders, but it was neatly combed back behind his ears. His face was scrubbed clean with a touch of summer tan in his cheeks. His mouth was small, round, and constantly in motion.

For some reason Pepper expected that his eyes would be blue or maybe green . . . and was surprised to see they were dark brown. Those eyes danced on the horizon, then shot a glance at the sky, then toward Pepper, then straight ahead at a hummingbird that paused in midair only a couple of feet in front of him.

Pepper found herself scooting through the tall grass to catch up with the boy. She was wearing a bright peach-colored dress with a wide white cotton belt, and a straw hat was pushed back on her head. She carried a closed parasol in her right hand that she used as a walking stick as she hurried along.

This is a beautiful child. He's so alert, so active! But he could get hurt out here. Where are his parents? He must have wandered off. Perhaps they're back in the trees. I'll just watch him for a while. I'm sure they won't mind. He's so adorable! He acts like he doesn't even see me.

The little boy seemed about three years old, but he never turned to really look at Pepper directly. Finally he stopped running and picked up a stick. Holding it in his chubby little right hand, he swung it wildly through the green weeds, causing the immature heads of wild oats to fly up into the blue sky.

A gentle, cool breeze swept up from the slope of the rolling hills forming a wave in the weeds. The little boy threw the stick, ran to retrieve it, then threw it again. This game was repeated over and over across the crest of the mountain.

The little boy began to pick up speed as the downward slope increased, and Pepper wanted to call out for him to slow down, but she didn't say anything. Scanning ahead, she panicked when she spotted a cliff overlooking a mountain stream coursing through the rocks and boulders below.

This time she screamed at the boy, but he didn't seem to hear. It was as if she was not even in the scene. She ran fast now. The stubble and pebbles of the hillside ground into her bare feet. The little boy was completely out of control, stumbling down the steep hill toward the cliff, and she could hear him yell with fright.

"Throw yourself to the ground!" she cried.

But the boy continued to run.

Approaching the edge of the cliff at the same time as the little boy, Pepper slowed to keep herself from plunging off the edge into the distant stream and boulders below. She thought the little boy had stopped right at the cliff's edge, but then he lost his footing.

"Mother!" he shrieked in panic, reaching out his chubby little arm.

Pepper spun around to look for the boy's mother, but there was no one there. When she turned back, the boy had slipped over the edge. She lunged to reach his hand, but she felt only the tips of his fingers as they slipped through hers.

With absolute terror in his voice as he fell, he looked Pepper straight in the eyes and screamed, "Mother!"

The room was extremely dark. Her flannel gown was drenched with sweat, and the back of her head pounded with a deep, throbbing, mind-numbing pain. She knew her eyes were open, but she lay there for a long time trying to remember.

Where am I?

How did I get here?

What happened to my head?

Where's April?

Was there a fight? Did someone hit me with a chair?

Stack? Where's Stack. Why didn't he pull them off me?

Tap? Did I get shot? Was it Beckett? No . . . he's dead.

Where's Tap?

The boy . . . oh, Lord . . . the little boy again. I still couldn't save him! Lord . . . I couldn't do anything about it. I really couldn't! You've got to believe me. Please believe me.

Pepper began to sob and was surprised to feel tears roll off her cheeks and onto the pillowcase beside her head. Reaching to her head, she felt bandages wrapped tight against her hair.

Lord, why do I keep dreaming of that little boy? I don't even know who he is.

She could see a dim light filter through the curtains of what looked like an extremely tall window.

Where am I?

Oh, Lord, I don't even know where I am!

Pepper began to cry again, and this time she couldn't stop.

She cried because of the intense pain.

She cried because she felt alone and lost.

She cried because the little boy had called her "Mother."

It seemed to her that she cried for hours.

Then a tall door opened, and a soft-burning lamp entered the room, followed by a blue flannel-robed arm and a brown-skinned, wide-eyed, wide-faced woman with long, black hair.

"Señora . . . are you awake?"

Pepper wanted to sit up and see clearly who it was, but her head felt as if it weighed five hundred pounds.

"Lie still, Señora. You are hurt very bad, I think."

Pepper tried to wipe her eyes on the bed sheet. Instantly the woman set the lamp by the bed and began to wipe Pepper's face with a damp cloth.

"Who are you?" Pepper asked.

"Oh, I am Rebecca Maria. I work here."

"Where am I?"

"Why, you are in the governor's house, of course."

"In Denver?"

"Yes, yes, it is the truth. Lie still. The doctor . . . he said you must not roll your head to the right or to the left. It could be very dangerous."

"What happened? How did I get here?"

"You must have forgotten the carriage wreck. A bear spooked the horses, and your husband could not keep it in control. You were thrown out and hit your head on a rock."

"My husband? Where's Tap? Where is he?"

"Who?"

"Eh . . . my husband . . ."

"You mean Mr. Dillard? Don't worry. He is all right. He only had a bad cut on his neck."

Dillard! Dillard shoved me out of that wagon! He tried to kill me. That was no cut on his neck.

"Yes . . . yes . . . where is, eh, Mr. Dillard?"

"I, too, am surprised. He said he would sit up with you, but he must have grown tired and laid down in the next room. I will go get him for you."

"No, that's . . . you don't . . ."

"Remember," Rebecca Maria instructed, "do not move your head, or you will vomit again."

"Again?"

"That is the third set of linens and the fourth nightgown."

"What?"

"I'll be right back."

Three sets of linens? Nightgowns? How long have I been here? Pepper stared up at the shadows flickering across the high ceiling. Within a minute Rebecca Maria returned, scooting across the hardwood floor.

"He is not there. He must have . . . Maybe he was worried and went out for the doctor."

And maybe he didn't give a buffalo chip whether I lived or died. A grieving widower could grab a sympathy contract.

"Don't worry. I will sit up with you," Rebecca Maria promised.

"Normally, I wouldn't want anyone to lose sleep over me . . . but I would really appreciate it if you stayed."

"Your gown is wet. Can I get you another?"

"It's all right. I can . . . Rebecca Maria, did you say this is my third gown?"

"Fourth."

"But I only brought one. Where did I get—"

"The governor's wife had several extras, and I wash them out and dry them by the fire."

"Did you find my gown in my things?"

"Oh, no. I was in the kitchen when they brought you in. Your husband placed you in the bed, I think. Of course, I've been the one to change you since then."

Dillard? Oh, sure, Dillard stripped me down! It figures.

"The doctor was with your husband. He is a very good doctor, I think. He looks after the governor's family."

"What time is it? Is it late?"

"I believe it is after midnight. But you have been asleep for a very long time. I was worried you might never wake up. They brought you in yesterday evening before dark."

"Yesterday? Did they have the dance already?"

"Oh, no. It was postponed . . . because of your accident, I think. It will be tomorrow night downstairs in the ballroom, but I heard them say you will not be allowed to attend."

Well, girl, that's one way to get out of this. That's the best news I've had in days.

Rebecca Maria added some wood to the fire that glowed in a small white brick fireplace at the end of the room. Then she returned with a fresh gown. She didn't bother asking Pepper, but began to patiently tug the soaked one off.

After a sponge bath, she gently pulled a fresh yellow cotton gown on Pepper.

"Is that better?"

"Oh, yes. I can't thank you enough. I've never in my life had someone help me like this."

"Besides your husband, you mean?"

"Oh . . . yeah."

Rebecca Maria then brought Pepper a drink of water and held her head by lifting the thick down pillow as she drank.

"The doctor says you are not to eat until he arrives in the morning. He's afraid it would cause you to vomit again."

The Mexican maid pulled a high-back chair next to the bed and sat down facing Pepper.

"You go ahead and sleep," she encouraged Pepper. "I will sit here."

"I'll be all right now. You have taken very good care of me. You can go back to bed," Pepper urged.

"No, no. I would not sleep for worry over you."

"Worry over me?"

"Oh, yes. If you have changed a woman's gown many times, you begin to feel like you know her quite well."

Pepper could feel her face flush.

"For instance, I know that you were once knifed just under your shoulder blade on the right side of your back."

"Well, I guess I've got no secrets from you." Pepper tried to smile.

"Did someone try to rob you? I am always afraid to walk across town in the dark."

"Oh, no. There was this girl working at the dance hall, and she . . ."

Pepper watched as Rebecca Maria's eyes grew wide.

"Señora! You have gone into one of those horrible dance halls? A woman like you should never go there!"

"Oh . . . it was years ago. Before I ever met . . . eh, Mr. Dillard. Anyway, you don't want to know about all of that."

The maid rocked herself back and forth in the straight-backed chair. "You should try to rest."

"Yes, you're right. I will." Pepper closed her eyes. "But I'm afraid it will be rather boring for you."

"Watching you is not boring." Rebecca Maria smiled. "You talk in your sleep."

Pepper's eyes flashed open. "Talk? Really? What do I say?"

"Oh, you ramble on and on making no sense at all. In your dreams you are mad at Señor Dillard. Then you are angry with a Señor Tap. And then you yell at a Señor Andrews. Are you mad at all men?"

"Oh . . . I . . . I have no idea why I say those things."

"You really make no sense at all. Talking about a blond-headed little boy. You have children yes?"

She can tell. Can't she? "Eh . . . no. No, I don't have any. Do you?"

"Señora, I am not married. Perhaps one day. Still you make no sense at all until you began mumbling about your Jesus."

"My Jesus?"

"Yes, you called to Him often, and it seemed like after you called to Him, you were able to sleep more soundly for a while."

"Well, I didn't know I had called to Jesus, but I imagine I did. Who else could someone call to at a time like this?"

For several minutes neither said anything. Pepper closed her eyes again and tried to think of something besides the throbbing at the back of her head.

"Rebecca Maria . . . I think I am falling asleep."

"Good night, Señora. I will be right here if you need me."

The last thing Pepper remembered seeing were the gentle brown eyes of the governor's maid sitting in the chair beside the bed.

When she opened her eyes again, daylight had flooded the room, and there was a tray with a cup of steaming tea and several pieces of fried bread.

A heavy-set man in long coat and tie peered at her over the top of small wire-rimmed spectacles.

"Oh . . . you're awake. Very good, very good. Now would you look straight at my eyes. Yes . . . Yes, this is good. Much clearer . . . much, much clearer."

"Who are you?" Pepper asked.

"Dr. Jamison." He nodded. "I will check back on you later in the day."

"Thanks, Doc. Eh," Pepper stammered, "do I owe you some money?"

"Hardly. The governor has taken care of everything. Rebecca Maria can send for me if you need anything. Now your husband is outside and wants desperately to talk to you. I'll send him in."

If he really wanted to talk to me, he would have stayed here last night.

"Rebecca Maria, stay in the room when Mr. Dillard comes in. Please don't leave me alone with him."

"What? Señora, why would—"

"Please," Pepper begged. "It's very important!"

"I will stay."

"*Gracias.*"

"*De nada.*"

Carter Dillard wore a long coat and black tie, and he carried his silk hat in his hand as he entered the room.

"Well," he said smiling, "how's my girl this morning? I was certainly worried. The doctor said that everything will be—"

"Cut the speech, Dillard. You got me to Denver. Isn't that what you wanted?"

Turning to Rebecca Maria, he nodded. "That will be enough. I'll take care of my wife now. You may leave . . . Go on . . . It's not necessary for you . . . Please, leave now! *¿Habla ingles?*"

"She's not going."

"What?"

"I asked Rebecca Maria not to leave me alone with you."

"Why?"

"'Cause you shoved me out of the carriage."

"Pepper, really!" Then he turned to the maid. "She has really taken a severe blow to the head. She's totally incoherent. The doctor gave me no indication that—"

"Dillard, listen to me, and listen carefully. As soon as I am physically able, I'm going to get up out of this bed and catch a stagecoach back to McCurley's. In the meantime, you can have your charade and your Governor's Ball and your railroad contracts and whatever. Just leave me out of it. I would prefer it if you never came back into this room again."

Carter Dillard glanced nervously again at the Mexican maid and then back to Pepper.

"But I don't . . . you can't . . . ," he stammered. "Rebecca Maria, quickly run and see if you can catch the doctor. I believe she has taken a turn for the worse. She doesn't even seem to know who I am!"

"She knows who you are, I think. But I do not know who you are. I will stay with the señora."

"You will what?" Dillard fumed. "I told you to get out of here, and I mean it!" He opened his topcoat revealing the .45 holstered at his hip.

"That's right, Rebecca Maria, Dillard's very good at beating up and threatening women. If you want to go, please do. Just don't get yourself hurt," Pepper offered.

"I am not without my own defenses. No, I think I will stay. The governor asked that I take care of the señora. I would not be doing him a service to abandon her now."

"This is ridiculous. I won't stand for it! I'll see the governor about this. He'll fire you immediately!"

"Yes, do that," Pepper added, "and when you do, please ask him to come and talk to me privately. I have many things to tell him."

Dillard stomped to the door, then spun, and came back toward Pepper.

Rebecca Maria stepped between Dillard and the bed. "I think the señora needs some rest now."

Shoving the maid aside, Dillard shouted at Pepper, "You mess this deal up, and you'll wish you would have died from that fall.

Do you understand? And you won't be the only one who has to pay. Your Mexican friend here will suffer too!"

Pepper glanced across the sunlit room. "Rebecca Maria, are you hurt?"

"*¿Este hombre malo no es su esposo?*"

"No."

"Pepper, did you hear me!" Dillard's face flushed red.

"Everyone in the governor's house heard you."

"Look," he sneered lowering his voice, "I'll stay out of this room, and you make sure the governor stays out too. In two days I'll be done with the negotiations, and then for all I care, you can go to . . ." Dillard heard someone knock at the bedroom door.

He turned and swung open the door to find the governor's wife standing with a newspaper in her hand and a worried look on her face.

"Is everything all right, Mr. Dillard? I thought I heard shouting."

"Yes . . . yes . . . I was just . . . a little excited to find my wife so alert."

"Oh, good. Well, there's a man at the front door who says that he must see you at once. I believe the name is Pardee. Mr. Pardee. He says it is quite urgent."

Dillard left the room in a huff, and the governor's wife stuck her head in the door. "Is everything all right, dear?"

"Yes, ma'am. Thanks for asking. But I think I will need Rebecca Maria to stay with me."

"Yes, of course. She will stay up here as long as you need her. Try to get some rest. And don't blame Mr. Dillard for being edgy. He's probably just very worried about your welfare." The governor's wife turned and headed down the hall.

Rebecca Maria opened the curtains to allow even more sunlight in the room and then came back to the bedside.

"Thank you for standing by me." Pepper smiled. "I have done nothing to deserve such loyalty. I'm afraid Dillard's threat was real. He can be a very vindictive man. We could both be hurt."

Rebecca Maria patted Pepper's hand between the palms of her

own. "I think perhaps that the señora has not had a very easy life."

"You sized that up right."

"I have not had an easy life either."

"It's a hard land out here." Pepper nodded.

"Oh, no, Señora, the land is very lovely. It is some of the people who are hard. Would you like to try to sit up a little today? Perhaps you would like to have me help you get dressed. You might feel better."

"I think I'll just lay right here for a while."

"Then I will sit here with you. The doctor said you should try to eat this bread. If it stays down, you can have some dinner." She tore off a small bite of fried bread and held it in front of Pepper's mouth.

"Oh, you don't have to feed me. I . . . I . . ."

"It is all right. I will feed you, and you will tell me about Mr. Tap."

Pepper chewed on the bite of sweet bread. "Mr. Tap?"

"You were talking in your sleep again last night. You were no longer angry with Mr. Tap, I think."

"It's quite a long story." Pepper sighed.

"I am a good listener. I hope he is nicer than Mr. Dillard."

Doctor Jamison stopped back around 2:00 P.M. Pepper was reclining on top of the bed covers, wrapped in a thick dark robe. Rebecca Maria warmed an iron in front of the fire, and a silver-and-black dress lay on a chair beside the bed.

"Oh my, you are making a splendid recovery! But you must take it easy. I cannot allow you to attend the dance tonight," he cautioned.

"Yes, I know, but Rebecca Maria thought I should try on the dress. It's new and I've never worn it."

"Have you been able to eat?"

"She eats everything I bring her." Rebecca Maria laughed. "Soon we will have nothing left for the governor's party."

"Well, if you can go through this afternoon and evening without losing your meal, then perhaps tomorrow you should try to walk around some."

"Doctor, when do you think I would be able to ride the stage? I don't want to be a burden on the governor."

"The stage? Oh, my . . . I don't think any woman should ever ride on a stage. The language—and the tobacco spit! Perhaps a carriage in a day or so."

By dark Pepper was wearing the silver dress, propped up on pillows at the head of the bed with a small quilt over her feet. She had removed the bandages from her head and had tucked her long blonde hair up in combs.

She sipped a cup of tea from a blue-patterned china cup. Rebecca Maria sat by her side also drinking tea.

"How many people are downstairs? It sounds like the whole city."

"Señora, there must be one hundred or so. There are several men from Washington, D. C. I think there are some senators here also. Do you wish you were at the party?"

"No, I wish I was back at McCurley's."

"I do not wish to be at the party either. But if you went to the party, I think the men would all chase you."

"Only until they got close enough to see the bruises. I look best when the lighting isn't very good."

"The señora is a very beautiful lady. Your yellow hair is just like the sunlight!"

"My hair . . . Rebecca Maria . . . you have that beautiful long, black hair. I have often wondered what I would look like with enchanting hair like yours. What do you think?"

"I think the señora has lost her senses." She laughed.

There was a quiet knock, and Rebecca Maria stepped toward the door.

"Tell Dillard I will not see him!" Pepper insisted.

After a hushed conversation at the barely opened door, the maid closed it quickly and returned to Pepper's side.

"That was Mr. Dillard. He's going to bring the governor up to check on your health."

"What did you tell him?"

"He didn't ask me. He just said they would be up in a few minutes. And that you should look presentable."

"I don't want to see them. I don't want to see either of them!"

"I think perhaps the señora should talk to the governor. You should tell him the truth. Tell him who Dillard is and how he is treating you."

"I can't do that . . . because everyone would say that the blow to my head has confused my mind. And if I did convince them I was telling the truth, Dillard would find a way to track me down and kill me—and you!"

"I will tell them you are too ill to visit with them."

There was another knock at the door.

"No, no. Let them in, but you stay in here with me."

Both the governor and Carter Dillard wore long dress coats and stiff ruffled shirts. The governor held a silk top hat in his hand.

"Mrs. Dillard! What a beautiful dress. It will be our loss that you cannot join us tonight."

"Thank you, Governor. I'm sorry this has happened."

"Well, thank goodness, you are recovering so rapidly from that rather nasty accident. Do I understand that your head feels better?"

"Yes. Thank the Lord."

"Pepper, dear," Dillard began, "I was just telling the governor that—"

"Mr. Governor," Pepper interrupted, "I want to say that my recovery is due to the excellent care given me by Rebecca Maria."

"Yes, we think she is a special girl." The governor smiled at the maid.

"As I was saying, I—," Dillard began again.

"I'm afraid I'll need her tonight and tomorrow as well. I hope this is not a burden to you."

"Oh, no, my dear. Rebecca Maria, you will stay by Mrs. Dillard's side until she fully recovers."

"Yes, sir." The maid turned slightly and winked at Pepper.

"As I was trying to say," Dillard asserted, "Governor, I wonder if it would be permissible for me to talk to my wife in private. The matter is . . . well, discreet."

"Certainly. Come on, Rebecca Maria. We should let—"

A heavy, insistent knock froze everyone in place. The maid scurried to answer the bedroom door. She stepped out into the hall and quickly returned.

"Governor! It is an emergency."

"Who is it?"

"He did not give me his name. He is with Mr. Whitney, and he says you are about to execute an innocent man. He insists on talking with you."

"Tonight?"

"Yes, right now."

"Oh, all right. It's that Billingsly matter I was telling you about, Dillard."

"My . . . eh, my word! Do you mind if I join in on this? It was a horrible crime."

"By all means, come on. Rebecca Maria, we will be in the library if anyone is looking for us."

"Yes, sir."

"Mrs. Dillard, it is with regret that we must hurry off. You still owe me a dance someday, young lady."

"I will keep my word, Governor."

"Yes . . . yes, that will be very nice. Mr. Dillard, if you will go downstairs and get Judge Rankin, I'll meet you in the . . ."

Their voices faded as the two men hurried out of the bedroom into the hall. The door swung closed behind them.

"I think the governor will miss his own ball," Rebecca Maria commented. She fluffed up a pillow behind Pepper. "Would you like me to go down and fetch you some refreshments from the party?"

"Oh, yes! I'm very hungry."

"Will you be all right by yourself?"

"Yes. Give me my valise."

"You mean the little revolver, don't you?"

Pepper smiled. "You think you know all about me."

"No. I think you are a lady who has so many secrets you cannot remember all of them yourself." She handed Pepper the small handgun.

"Go on. Go get plenty of refreshments for both of us."

Rebecca Maria stood at the door. "I will lock it behind me, no? All this talk about hanging killers gives me the chills!"

Pepper sat up and stretched her arms. "Who were you talking about? Who is the man condemned to die?"

"I think it is the Indian lawyer."

"Who?"

"The Comanche lawyer—Mr. Eagleman. It was in all the papers how he shot Mr. Billingsly in the back."

"Eagleman? Wade Eagleman?" Pepper gasped.

"Yes, yes. Do you know him?"

"No! I mean . . . remember I told you that long story? Who was the man at the door just now? Was that Eagleman?"

"Oh, no. Eagleman is in jail. That was a friend of his and Mr. Whitney, the governor's secretary."

"Did you know the other man?"

"No, I have never seen him."

"Did he wear a brown leather vest with Indian beadwork above the left pocket and an old gray hat sloping at the front and a—"

"Oh, no. He was wearing a suit and bright gold vest. He was quite handsome. Perhaps he is part Comanche himself. Why do you ask?"

"My Tap came to Denver to get Eagleman to help him."

"I'm afraid Mr. Eagleman is the one who needs the help."

"And Tap would try to help him. Did the man at the door have a black mustache?"

"Yes, but fifty men in the ballroom have black mustaches. I don't think it could have been your Tap."

"Did his eyes dance, Rebecca Maria? When you talked to him, did his eyes dance in such a way that made your heart beat faster?"

The Mexican maid blushed.

"It did! Didn't it? That was him. That was my Tap!"

"Shall I go get him, Señora? I will be very cautious."

"No! No. Don't you see? I must leave at once. Order a carriage to the back of the house. I will pack my things. He can't find me here!"

"But . . . you hate Mr. Dillard and have been wanting to get back to Mr. Tap. Now that he might be here, you want to run?"

Lord, why doesn't this make sense to anyone but me?

6

Most of the patrons at the Pearly Gate Dance Hall quickly resumed their drinking, dancing, gambling, and various other forms of debauchery the moment Tap eased the bartender back down to his feet and turned to face the woman dressed in purple velvet.

"Rena . . . I thought . . ."

"Around here I'm called Lena."

"You work here?" Tap surveyed the room. Several men's hands rested on their holstered handguns as they watched him.

"You might say that. You haven't changed much."

"You wouldn't believe the changes," Tap replied.

An argument at a poker table in the back corner of the room caused them both to look in that direction for a moment. Then Tap pushed his gray hat back and shook his head. "You look good, Rena. Maybe the makeup's a little thick, and the dress is much too revealing, but you're still the prettiest thing Globe City ever saw. This doesn't seem like the right kind of place for you to work."

"Don't think you're the first cowboy to feed me that line, Mr. Tapadera Andrews. Besides, technically, I don't work here."

"How's that?"

"I own the place."

"You own the Pearly Gate?"

"Me and a silent partner. I run the operation."

"Well, now, that's quite a distance from being a bank manager's wife in Arizona."

A loud slap and a curse punctuated their conversation. A short, bald-headed man with a handlebar mustache got smacked along-side the head by a dance-hall girl who was almost as wide as she was tall. At the same time three Welsh miners began singing a Celtic tune near the bar.

Rena shrugged. "It's not boring." Tap felt her warm, soft hand link fingers with his. "Come on, we have a lot of talking to do!" She tugged him through the crowd toward a back room.

"Look, Rena . . . I don't want to go back there. What I want is some information."

A wide smile broke across her painted lips. "This is my office, not my bedroom. We can't talk out here. It's too noisy."

Stepping into the back room at the Pearly Gate was like walk-ing into a different world. A big oak rolltop desk hovered near a lace-curtained window. Oil paintings lined the far wall above a standing globe and black leather couch.

Rena beckoned for him to join her as she sat down at one end of the sofa. "I really am relieved to find that you're not in jail in Yuma."

"No thanks to you. Rena, why did you run off? Where did you go?"

"Why are you staring at me like that?" she asked.

"Like what?"

"Like you're looking at a ghost or something. I . . . know I look older. There's nothing left that's prim or proper, is there?"

He stood up and paced the office. "I didn't say a word about that."

"Tap, those big brown eyes of yours read like an open book. You never could hide anything you felt."

"You're avoiding the subject."

"You mean, where did I go after I shot Howard?"

"Yeah, I thought you went to get the sheriff."

"I thought you were the one going after the law."

"Me?" Tap exclaimed. "Why would I do that? You were the one who shot your husband."

"Precisely. So you had nothing to fear."

"Wait a minute." Tap stopped his prowling and stared at Rena. "You fled because you thought I was going to turn you over to the authorities?"

"I was terrified. I thought they'd hang me. Or worse, send me to prison for the rest of my life. I thought you'd be all right because you hadn't done anything. So I ran."

"Where'd you go?"

"To Mexico at first. I was so scared, Tap. I don't know why I shot him. I never did anything like that before then."

"Before then?"

"I've done a lot of things since then that I never figured I'd do. Anyway, at that moment it was like I just lost all control—control of my actions, control of my judgments, control of my morals. Everything was gone, and I ran."

Tap waved his hand to animate his words. "Meanwhile I faced a trial for a murder I didn't commit. Didn't that bother you?"

"I was all messed up. Most every day I spent drunk down in Dante. When I thought about it, I just knew you would tell them the truth. Then they'd let you go and come lookin' for me. Why didn't you tell them I shot him?"

"Because Howard was a jerk who used to whip you with his belt and then lock you in the bedroom closet while he went out chasing women." Tap could see the smudges in Rena's makeup where the tears began to trickle down from the corners of her eyes. "Besides, I didn't think they would convict me either. In the end lots of folks thought I might have killed you as well."

"What?"

"Yeah. When you disappeared, they searched the canyons and draws for your body. So I went to prison, and you went into business in Colorado."

"Well . . . at first I just knew they would ride over the border and arrest me. So I . . . I was really insane. I found someone who wasn't afraid to use a gun. He would be my protector."

Tap sighed and looked into Rena's red-streaked eyes. "So you latched onto Victor Barranca? That's worse than being with Howard."

"Yes. It's a choice I have often regretted. Vic did say that he knew you."

"You might say that."

"Well, I stayed in Mexico until last summer. Some man wanted to hire Vic to come up to Colorado and do some work. So I figured it was safe, and I—"

"Safe because I was in prison for your crime."

Rena stared at Tap for a moment. Her eyes looked sad. For the first time Tap realized that the room felt cold and smelled of stale cigar smoke.

"Yes . . . that was part of it. I came to Denver with Vic, and after several weeks the man who hired him . . . he . . . well, he seemed to take a special interest in me. So he bought this business and said if I would run the place, he'd share the profits with me as long as no one knew he owned it."

"Mighty nice of him. A real generous soul."

"Oh, he gets paid back. He doesn't do anything without getting paid back."

"So here you are in Denver makin' money left and right?"

"I get by. But in this place, you never know who will get shot in the back on any given night. Besides, hanging around with Victor Barranca is like carrying a lantern into a room full of black powder. There's a tendency to live one day at a time."

"The saloon is yours. Why don't you dump Barranca?"

"That's easy for a man with a gun on his hip to say. I've kicked him out a dozen times in the past three months, but he doesn't go any farther than the girls down the hall. Enough of that . . . I've got a lifetime to be depressed. What about Mr. Tapadera Andrews? What are you doing at the Pearly Gate? How did you know where to find me?"

"Well, it's a long story, but the core of it is that I came to town to talk to a lawyer about how to clear things up in Arizona. I wanted to get that settled so I wouldn't have bounty hunters showing up at my ranch every other day."

"You have a ranch?"

"I've got a ranch, a fiancée, and a future. But not with that Arizona matter hangin' over my head."

She jumped to her feet. "Wait a minute! Are you trying to tell me Tap Andrews is engaged to get married? Did you find a rich widow or what?"

"I found a lady who was as tired of runnin' and pretendin' as I was. Anyway, I came here to talk to a friend and found him in jail scheduled to hang for a crime he didn't commit."

Rena walked over to her desk, picked up an empty ink bottle, and turned back to Tap. "So what does that have to do with me?"

"Well, I didn't know it was you. I was told there was a Lena workin' at the Pearly Gate that knew where I could find a certain man. I didn't come here lookin' for you."

She opened a drawer and put the bottle inside. "For whom?"

"Victor."

"Yeah . . . it figures. Eagleman! Your lawyer friend is Wade Eagleman."

"Yep. So I guess what I'm sayin' . . . Rena, is Barranca around? I want to talk to him."

Rena stepped over to a small oval mirror and brushed back her raven hair with her fingers. The curls tumbled past her shoulders. "I should have known. It was kind of fun thinkin' about old times. Tap Andrews breaking out of prison to be with the woman he shielded from a murder arrest. Sounds like a dime novel, doesn't it?" She wiped the corners of her eyes with a linen hankie that she pulled from her laced sleeve.

"Barranca. Where's Victor?"

"I haven't seen him for hours, but if he's still at the Pearly Gate, he'll be upstairs with one of the girls."

"With you down here?"

"It doesn't bother me. Nothing bothers me anymore except knowing that you were in the Arizona Territorial Prison. I'm really glad you're out."

"I've got to talk to Barranca about that Billingsly killin'."

"He won't want to see you. He's been staying out of sight for the past several weeks on orders from his employer."

"Did Victor shoot Billingsly?"

"I know nothing about anything. That way I'll never have to appear in court."

"Which room is he in?"

"It's not that easy to take him. Three fellas, bounty hunters, came lookin' for him a few days ago, and he shot all three. 'Course, shootin' like that doesn't make the newspapers. You ever heard of the Lane brothers?"

"Jim-One and Jim-Two—that gang?"

"Yeah. He killed them all."

"That isn't sayin' much. I've known porcupines that are quicker than those three. Which room is he in?"

"Well, first off, he's taken to posting a guard at the bottom of the stairs. So unless a man comes upstairs with one of the girls, they're not allowed past the guard. But besides that, I don't know whose room he'll be in tonight. Our room is the big one at the end of the hall. Maybe he's there."

"You can walk me past the guard. I need a favor, Rena."

"So you can kill Barranca?"

"I don't want to kill anybody. I just want to talk. Just show me the room."

"But I told you I don't know—"

"I don't believe that for a moment." He lifted his gray hat and brushed his fingers through thick brown hair. Then he put his right hand on her shoulder. "If he's your man, then you know exactly who he's cheatin' with."

Rena reached down and brushed her dress off as if she were about to be introduced at the Governor's Ball. Then, not looking up at Tap, she spoke softly. "Sarah. If he's not in our apartment, he'll be with Sarah. She's in 8."

"Will you walk me up there?"

"I'll walk you past the guard, but I won't stay around and watch the shooting."

"Look, I told you, I'm not goin' to—"

"Tap, he'll shoot you on sight. He's told me that. You . . . Brannon . . . . the Earp brothers. He claims he'll shoot any of you that ever shows up in Denver."

"Same old Victor. It's nice to know that some folks remain the same. I'm glad to hear it's nothing personal."

"Come on, Mr. Engaged Rancherman, I owe you a favor, but

I'm not sure this will be to your benefit . . . or mine." She slipped her arm into Tap's and walked him back out into the saloon and dance hall.

A piano banged away at some forgotten tune while the shouts and laughter in the crowded room numbed the mind as quickly as the watered-down drinks. Rena seemed to glide through it all, graciously tossing out words and smiles like a queen in a parade.

The man in the straight-back wooden chair at the bottom of the stairs stood as they reached the landing area. He looked Andrews over from head to foot, resting his eyes on the Colt .44.

"Evenin', Miss Lena!" he greeted, chewing on a toothpick.

"Bobby, I've got a personal question for you," she said softly. "Is Vic at home, or did he go visitin'?"

The man with a bushy black beard raised his eyebrows. "I do believe he's, ah . . . you know . . . out visiting."

"Thanks, Bobby."

"Yes, ma'am." He tipped his hat to her and sat back down.

Reaching the unnumbered door at the end of the hall, Rena turned and whispered, "I'll go in just to make sure he's not here at our place."

She stepped inside the door and closed it behind her.

What if this is a setup? What if Barranca's really in there and she knows it? What if he swings open the door with guns blazing? Why should I trust her?

With the opening of the door, Tap reached for his revolver.

Startled at his drawn .44, Rena grabbed his sleeve and pulled him inside the room. "Relax! He's not here."

"Then I'll head down to room 8. Is that room laid out like this one?"

"Not hardly! It's small. The bed is on the right, behind the door. You can't see who's there when you first walk in unless you look at the tiny, round mirror above the dresser. Of course, if the lamp's turned off and the curtain's drawn, you won't see much of anything."

"Will he try to crawl out the window and get down to the street?"

"Maybe. But he's got a room full of friends down below. All he needs to do is stir them up, and you wouldn't stand a chance. There's no one in this building that will come rescue you, Tap—not even me. You could get shot down and dumped in a canyon like those Lane brothers. No one in the city would know. And few would care."

"Well, I don't aim to have anyone get killed."

"Yeah, you keep sayin' that. But somehow it feels different to me."

"And this Sarah—is she the type to stab me when my back is turned?"

"If she takes a mind to it, Sarah will stab you when you're lookin' straight at her with a gun in your hand."

"Does Barranca still have a cross-the-body holster?"

"Yeah."

"And does he carry six cartridges in the cylinder?"

"You know him well."

"Only from the sights of a gun."

"So I guess I'll wait here and see which one of you comes through the door."

"I've got to find a way to get Wade a postponement. Killing Barranca certainly won't accomplish that."

"And I say only one of you will walk out of that room alive."

"Which one are you hopin' for?"

Rena took the ribbons out of her raven hair and began to comb it. "Well, if I was smart I'd have sent you away twenty minutes ago and never brought you up here. But it's obvious I'm pretty dumb when it comes to choosing men. Barranca's a violent, immoral drunk. And Tap . . . well, he's impetuous, stubborn, exciting, and gentle with the ladies.

"But, you see, as long as I own this establishment, Barranca will stay with me and protect me, whether I want the protection or not. And Tap? Well, he will kiss me tenderly on the lips and ride off into the mountains . . . or desert . . . or canyons. I will lose and I will win no matter what happens. But I do believe that you will try to keep both of you alive, at least for a while." She paused her combing enough to turn around and look Tap in the eyes. "Perhaps . . . perhaps you can do it."

He pulled his Colt .44-40 and slipped another bullet into the chamber. Then he stepped toward the door and slid his hand around the cold brass door handle. He glanced back at Rena. For a moment he thought about kissing her.

But he didn't.

Walking quietly down the dimly lit, stale-smelling hall, he stopped at the room marked 8. Placing his ear to the oak door, he paused.

Lord, I've got a few hours before I have to shoot Wade out of jail. I sure hope this is going to work.

He rapped on the door with the barrel of the revolver.

After some noisy confusion, a weak female voice answered, "Yes, what is it?"

"Sarah?" Andrews called. "There's a man down at the bar that wants to see you."

"I'm busy!"

"This old boy's carrying a silver-handled cane," Tap called.

He heard a man's voice curse. "Silver cane? That's Masterson! What's he doin' in Denver? Go see what he wants, and don't tell him I'm up here. You understand?"

"But, Victor, I don't want to go see some old—"

Tap heard a loud slap of an open hand striking bare flesh.

"Ow! I'm goin'! I'm goin'! You had no call to do that."

With his gun still drawn, Tap slipped down the hall and around the corner. He waited until he heard the door squeak open. A dark-haired girl buttoned the sleeves of her dress and descended the staircase.

He stepped softly to the door. Sarah had not pulled it completely closed. Silently shoving the door open a couple of inches, Tap glanced at the mirror above the dresser. He could see a reflection of a shirtless Victor Barranca strapping on his bullet belt and holster around his waist.

Quickly sliding into the room, Tap pointed the cocked .44 at Barranca's head.

"Drop the gun belt, Victor!" he shouted.

"Andrews! What the—"

"Drop it!"

"I heard you broke out of A. T. P., but I hoped the Mojaves had buried you alive in the Arizona desert!"

Tap stepped closer to Barranca. "The belt. Drop it on the floor."

"If I drop this, how am I going to draw and shoot you in the gut?"

Holding the gun at Barranca's head, Tap walked right up to the side of the bed. "You don't have any choice. I've got two hundred grains of lead that will pass through your thick skull before your finger ever feels that trigger. And you know for a fact, Victor, that I won't hesitate to pull the trigger."

Barranca stood and began to fumble at the buckle of his bullet belt. Suddenly he growled, "Then pull it!" He reached across his stomach to draw his revolver.

The barrel of Tap's .44 slammed across the forehead of Victor Barranca, whose revolver dropped to the blue quilt wadded up on the floor. Barranca staggered back and collapsed on the bed.

Andrews retrieved the revolver and shoved it into his belt. Then he walked around to the far side of the bed so that he could watch the unconscious Barranca and the door at the same time.

Real smart, Tap. Victor can't talk much when he's cold-cocked like that. She'll be back in here in no time at all and no tellin' how many with her.

Jamming his Colt back into his holster, Tap struggled to lift Barranca to his shoulder. Staggering to the door, he peered cautiously down the hall, and then scooted to Rena's room. She was still at the mirror combing her hair when he entered.

"I didn't hear any shots! Is he dead?"

"Nope. Just sleepin'."

"Where's Sarah?"

"Downstairs lookin' for Masterson."

"Bat? Bat's here?"

"Nope. Neither is his brother Ed. But she thinks one of them's down there."

"What are you goin' to do with Vic?"

"Wake him up."

"In here?"

"That's better than sittin' down there waitin' for Sarah to return."

"But he'll know that I . . ."

"Go on down and entertain the guests. That way no one will know you have anything to do with it." Tap dumped Barranca onto the top of the bed. The gunman lay sprawled out on his stomach with his arms draped to the floor on the far side of the bed.

"Bobby will tell him. I thought my life was already complicated. If you don't kill Barranca, he'll kill me."

"Not if I'm around," Tap asserted.

He heard someone run down the hall. Then there was a soft rap at the door.

"Vic? It wasn't Masterson at all. Someone just playin' a joke. Come on back."

She rapped again. "Vic? Are you in there?"

Tap started toward the door, but Rena motioned him to stand back out of sight. He noticed that she had removed her heavy makeup and gaudy jewelry.

Holding her finger over her lips as a signal for him to be silent, she opened the doorway a couple of inches.

"What do you want with Vic?" she growled.

"Oh . . . Miss Lena! . . . well, I thought . . . I heard you were . . . I mean, I was checkin' to see if Vic was all right!" Sarah stammered.

"Of course, he's all right. I can take care of him just fine. Now I suggest if you want to still have a job tomorrow, you go downstairs and get to work."

"Eh . . . yes, ma'am. I was on my way. Oh . . . if he starts lookin' for his boots, they are in . . . my room," Sarah added with a guarded laugh.

"Good. I'll expect you to polish them before bringing them back."

"What? I didn't hire on to polish boots!" she protested.

"Just what exactly did you hire on to do?"

Sarah glared at her and then scurried off down the stairs.

Closing the door, Rena turned back to Tap.

"Did I catch a little lack of sisterly love?" he chided.

"The competition in a place like this can be . . . deadly." Rena sighed.

"You look nice without all that war paint on your face."

"I knew you would say that, Andrews. Why do you think I took it off? And for pete's sake, stop staring at me. The shock must be over by now. Do you still want me to go downstairs and leave you with Barranca?"

"It's up to you. Do whichever is safer for you."

"Then I think I've decided to stay. It's too late for anything safe."

"I don't know what will happen when he wakes up."

"Neither do I. That's why I'm staying."

Cold water splashed on his face brought Barranca around. He discovered his hands tied behind him to the heavy oak bedpost. Tap Andrews sat beside him on a wooden stool, revolver in hand. Rena stood on the other side of the room by a basin of water that sat on a small rosewood table.

"I might have known Lena was in on this!" he grumbled.

"Rena didn't do anything but wipe your face and bandage that cut on your forehead. I forced her to bring me up here."

"Lena. Her name's Lena."

"Not to old friends like me," Tap informed him.

"I can holler and bring half the dance hall up here with guns drawn."

"You holler and you're dead."

"What do you want, Andrews? You haven't killed me yet, so you must want something. Well, whatever it is, I ain't givin' it to you. The way I figure it, you're goin' to kill me sooner or later, so I ain't givin' you nothin'."

"As much as you deserve it, I don't plan on killin' you," Tap replied.

"You got to. You turn me loose, and I'll shoot you. You know that for a fact."

"Maybe I'll just get you tossed into jail for the next eighty or one hundred years."

"What for?"

"How about shootin' Billingsly in the back?"

"They done convicted a man for that. They cain't try me for a crime they already hung a man for."

"He's not hung yet."

"Don't matter. I didn't do it."

"I've talked to a couple of boys who said that you did."

"Who?"

"Three Fingers Slim and Jacob Rippler. They told me you were here at the Pearly Gate."

"They what? I . . . eh, I never heard of them," Barranca stammered.

"Well, I think the two of them are pretty shrewd businessmen. It was surprising how talkative they became when I offered them more money for talkin' than you did for keepin' quiet."

"That's bull. They ain't got the guts to go against me. Besides, I wasn't close to the Club the night Billingsly was killed. I was right here with Lena, wasn't I, darlin'?"

"Why, certainly. Vic is such an adoring man he never ever leaves my sight. I know where he is absolutely twenty-four hours of every day, don't I, darlin'?"

"Lena! Don't play games. Tell Andrews where I was the night Billingsly was killed."

"Well, I'm not sure. It could have been with Sarah in 8 or Lucille in 12 or maybe Peggy Ann in 7."

"You ain't helpin', Lena. But it don't matter. You know you don't have nothin' that will change their minds down at the jail. Ain't that right, Mr. Tapadera Andrews?"

"I'm still workin' on it."

"You know, Andrews, I could never figure you out. You're dumb and you're slow. It beats me how you've lived so long. If I were you, I'd shoot me right now. Go down and bust out that Injun attorney friend of yours, then grab Lena-girl, and ride for the high country."

"If I were you, Vic, I wouldn't give him any suggestions!" Rena cautioned.

"But you ain't me, Lena. You don't know him at all. This

Tapadera here—he's a man who thinks even gunmen ought to follow some code of conduct. 'Yes, sir. There's got to be honor among shootists,' he says. Why, there ain't even honor among honest men! Old Tap there won't even shoot a man in the back, will ya? That's the best way to shoot 'em because they cain't return fire."

"That's why you shot Billingsly in the back?" Tap pressed. "'Cause you were afraid of gettin' yourself shot by some soft-skinned rich man?"

"It weren't the back. Them papers got it all wrong. I shot him straight on once in the heart and once in the neck," Barranca boasted. "And I shot him 'cause I was paid more money than you've ever seen."

Tap glanced over at Rena and raised his eyebrows.

"Well, Rena, maybe it's time to talk to the governor about postponing that hanging. Would you be willin' to tell what you just heard?"

"Yeah. I might need a good attorney like Eagleman myself someday."

"Lena! . . . there ain't anyone in this town who will believe you two. I've got important friends, you know."

"My name's Rena. And if you have such important friends, why have you been hiding down there in room 8 for weeks?"

"I'm sorry about Sarah. It won't happen again!" Barranca pleaded.

Rena walked over to him and shoved the purple silk scarf she had been twisting in her hand into Barranca's mouth and began to tie it behind his head.

"I'll kill you," he mumbled.

She turned back to Tap. "Well, cowboy, what do we do now? It looks like you're stuck with protecting me now. There is no way to get him down through that crowd to the street while he's kickin' and screamin'."

"There's some back stairs, aren't there?"

"No."

"No? There's got to be a back way out. What if you had a fire, an emergency?"

"The Pearly Gate has only one entrance. Sounds sort of Biblical, doesn't it?"

"Have you got a good lock for that walk-in closet?"

"Yes."

"We've got to lock him in there. I have to get to the governor's office and try to stop the hanging."

"It will be closed."

"I'll find someone around."

"Why not go see the governor himself?"

"He's out of town. Up at Hot Springs or something," Tap reported.

"He's back in town now."

"How do you know that?"

"There is nothin' that happens in state government that doesn't make its way to the Pearly Gate."

"I'll need you to come with me. He just might believe two witnesses to Barranca's confession."

"I know. But you can't go to the governor's house dressed like a driftin' drover. He's having a big ball tonight. Everyone will be wearin' their finest."

"Well, I got a new suit over at the hotel."

Rena pulled out a heavy coat as Tap rolled a bound-and-gagged Victor Barranca into the closet and tied him there.

"He might get out of there," she cautioned.

"I'll have to deal with that later. There's no time to do anything else. Are you willing to risk it, Rena?"

"Oh, I'm real brave as long as you're around. Besides, I've always wanted to know what it was like to lock a man in a closet."

"Well, how's it feel?"

"Real good! Real good. Now give me a little time to get the Pearly Gate situated to run awhile without me."

Tap walked slowly though the crowd and out the front door, not stopping to say anything to anyone. The cold night air caused him to tug down his hat and roll up his collar. He shoved his hands into the deep pockets of his long coat and found the open slot that allowed him to rest his right hand on the walnut handle of his holstered .44. He stepped back away from the red lantern that served as a guide to the Pearly Gate's front door.

Lord, this keeps gettin' more and more complicated. I just want to keep Wade from gettin' hung. I didn't plan to solve the Billingsly case.

And, Lord, take care of Pepper tonight. She's back there at McCurley's worried sick about me wonderin' when I'm comin' back . . . or if I'm comin' back. I surely pray that she's havin' a quiet time visitin' with folks and relaxin' in her room. Help her to be so busy tonight she doesn't think about me at all.

"You go to sleep?" Rena slipped her arm into his.

"I was thinkin' . . . about Pepper."

She pulled her hand away and shoved it into her pocket.

"She's really caught you, hasn't she?"

"It's a mutual feelin'."

"I often think about what would have happened if Harold hadn't stumbled upon us that night in Globe City."

"Yeah, you never know how close you are to an event that turns your life upside down."

It was after 9:00 P.M. when they finally walked up to the front door of the governor's house. Tap tried to straighten his tie. "Do I look as awkward as I feel in this suit?"

"I've seen gamblers lose a thousand dollars who looked happier than you. That vest is awful!"

"Thanks. That's reassuring," Tap groaned.

"Now pretend like you've been invited to a party."

"We're goin' to barge right in?" he asked.

The man with the badge at the governor's front door tipped his hat and held the door for them.

"We make a handsome couple, Mr. Andrews. Of course, if Victor gets loose, he'll shoot me when I return home. But then it just might be worth it."

One of the first men Tap spotted was the governor's secretary, Mr. Whitney. Tap approached the man and grabbed his shoulder.

"Did you present those papers to the governor?"

"Oh, yes. He came back from Hot Springs to review the case."

"What did he decide?"

"I don't think he's come to a conclusion."

"Can I talk to him? There's more evidence. Miss Rena and I heard a man confess—"

"At the Pearly Gate?" Whitney scowled, looking over the top of his glasses at Rena.

"Eh, ye-yeah, as a matter of fact," Tap stuttered.

"That hardly qualifies as hard evidence."

"Well, how about this," Rena added. "He said that Billingsly was really shot straight on twice—one shot in the neck and the other in the heart."

"And he was paid big money to do it," Andrews added.

"By whom? Who hired him?"

"He didn't say. Did Billingsly get shot from the front?"

"Eh . . . yes. That's what the examining doctor reported."

"But the papers said it was in the back."

"They didn't know what they were talking about. Someone with pull wanted a quick, easy case. That's why the paper said that," Whitney reported. "I'll take you upstairs to see the governor. This case has been bothering him."

They slid past the well-dressed guests and started up a wide staircase.

"The governor's up here visiting a house guest who had a nasty accident. We'll just wait. As soon as he comes out, I'll have you talk to him."

For several minutes Tap paced the hallway and Rena stood at the top of the stairway glancing down at the party.

Finally Tap burst out, "I don't want to seem disrespectful, Mr. Whitney, but if I don't get to present this to the governor pretty soon, Wade Eagleman will hang."

Without further hesitation, Andrews spun around and rapped insistently on the tall, white wooden door.

In a moment a Mexican maid with long, black hair stepped out into the hall.

7

Most times government matters move slowly:
Forms to fill out.
Committees to convene.
A dozen people to see.
Stiff wooden benches in the hallways that give you a backache after several hours of waiting.

For Tap that's exactly the way most of the day had gone.

Until now.

The governor now seemed almost anxious to postpone Eagleman's hanging after listening to Tap's and Rena's detailed account. He granted an immediate extension and sent authorities to the Pearly Gate to apprehend Victor Barranca for questioning.

While Rena mixed with the guests at the party, Tap continued the discussion with the governor.

"You really believe Eagleman is innocent?"

"Yes, sir, I do."

"Well, I haven't felt good about this all along. I keep thinking it might be the biggest mistake this state's made since Chivington's debacle out at Sand Creek. But I'm going to need a confession from the Barranca fellow or some hard evidence that will be enough to take him to trial." He paced the library with his arms behind his back. "Can we get those two drifters back to speak to the court?"

"I doubt if we could find them now. On the other hand, they might still be at the Seven Mile Saloon. But if they lied to the jury last time, they sort of destroyed their usefulness at stating the truth, haven't they?" Tap walked back and forth alongside the governor. His tie was loosened and his collar was unbuttoned.

"Yes . . . yes, I suppose. Still there's got to be some connection . . . some evidence . . . something!"

"Well, I'm goin' to find it. Wade's a friend of mine, and this just isn't fair. I don't think this country knows what to do with a successful Indian." Tap held his hat in his hand as he talked.

"I think you might have something there," the governor agreed. "Most folks think the Indians ought to play by our rules. Then when they get good at it, everyone is upset. That whole Billingsly matter went much too quickly from the start, and I couldn't figure out how to stop it. But I've got to have some confirmation."

The governor walked Tap and Rena to the front door of his house. "I'd appreciate it if you would stop by my office in the morning. We'll see if we learn anything from this Victor Barranca. Shall I send the authorities after those two witnesses?"

"Yes, sir, it won't hurt." Tap shook the governor's outstretched hand. "I'm mighty sorry for disturbing your party like this."

"Oh, no . . . no. Listen, Mr., eh, was it Andrews?"

"Yep."

"Well, Mr. and Mrs. Andrews, you're certainly invited to stay for the ball."

"No, actually we're not, eh . . . well, thanks anyway. But I want to go over to the jail and see if they'll let me report all this to Wade Eagleman."

"Yes, that's quite understandable. Good night then."

Tap tipped his hat, and he and Rena began to walk up the street. She slipped her arm into his.

"Mr. and Mrs. Andrews! What do you know about that!"

"Well, for one thing I'm glad Pepper's a hundred miles away!"

What am I doin'? I don't even want to be here. And I surely don't want a lady hanging on my arm! Lord, I need to get back to McCurley's. As soon as Wade gets out of jail, I'm haulin' out of here. Pepper's right. I should just leave this whole Arizona thing behind.

After a brief late-night stop to see a jubilant Wade Eagleman, Tap escorted Rena back toward the Pearly Gate.

"I suppose they've carried off Vic by now," Rena was saying.

Tap jammed his cold hands into the side pockets of his suit coat. "Unless he escaped that closet. I have a gut-level feelin' that I should have shot him."

"Has your gut-level feelin' ever been wrong?"

"Yep."

"When?"

"In a hotel down in Globe City."

"Will every conversation we have keep coming back to that?" she asked.

"Probably. It's the whole reason I'm in Denver."

"Tap, I don't think I can help you like you want me to. I know I should. I know that I owe you something . . . but I guess I'm thinkin' some of this tonight sort of pays you off. This cost me, Tap—this thing with Vic cost me, but he'll have to find me first."

Tap glanced through the dark night at Rena's soft blue eyes. "Find you?"

"I sold my share of the Pearly Gate."

"What do you mean, sold it? How? When?"

"At the governor's party. My silent partner was there, so I sold my part back to him."

"But . . . I didn't want you to have to—"

"Look, Tap, let's get some things straight," Rena lectured as they walked past a row of darkened shops. "I ran out on you in Globe City. It's been eating at me for years. Now I suddenly had a way to help you out. I don't regret doing it. I stood by you this time. I didn't run. But . . . I can't stick around here now. Vic will find a way to get out of jail. Then he'll get drunk and come slice me up. I'm not going to wait around for that. I helped you out. I've got more money than I came to town with. I've done all right."

"But the Pearly Gate . . . it was a—"

"It was a constant embarrassing disappointment to everything decent in me. And believe it or not, Tapadera Andrews, there is still a little decency left."

"So where are you headed?" Tap asked.

"San Francisco . . . Virginia City . . . who knows?"

"How about Globe City, Arizona?"

"I can't, Tap. You could serve prison time for me. I know that. But I can't do it. This is it, Tap. This is what I did for you. I helped you in Denver. You'll remember that, won't you?"

"I won't forget. But, look, you can't just skip out now. Not until we help Wade get out of jail. They might need us to give the judge a statement on what Vic said."

"I'll stay only if Vic's in jail."

Tap felt uneasy about going back into the Pearly Gate, but he buried his reluctance and held the door for Rena. The noisy, smoky warmth of the crowded saloon and dance hall came as sharp contrast to the clear, cold cleanness of the Denver night. One of the men met them before they made it halfway across the room.

"Miss Lena, the marshal was here lookin' for Vic! I thought they was goin' to close us down."

The man eyed Tap's suit and gold-braided vest.

This is the last time I wear a store-bought suit.

"It's all right, Rudy. This is Mr. Andrews, a friend of mine. He was in earlier. Remember? Did the marshal take Vic with him?"

"Nope."

"What?" she gasped.

"Well, they were too late. Vic left with Sarah about five minutes before the marshal and deputies got here. I thought he went out to find you."

"I should have shot him," Tap mumbled.

She took the man by the arm. "I need to tell Rudy a few things."

"I'll check upstairs," Tap told her. He scooted through the crowd.

The man at the bottom of the stairs glanced at Tap's eyes and stepped aside without saying anything. He climbed two stairs at a time with his suit coat pushed back and his hand on the handle of his Colt.

The room was empty, as was the closet. Other than the ropes and gag tossed on the floor, everything looked the same as earlier in the evening.

A few minutes later, Rena burst into the room with a rustle of petticoats and an aroma of lilac perfume.

"Did you get Rudy set up to run the place?" Tap asked.

"Yeah. He'll do all right—until Vic shows up. I'm leavin' right now, Tap. I can't stay here."

"Yeah, I figured that. But there won't be any stages or trains pulling out until mornin'."

"I'd rather take my chance at the train station than sit here and wait for Vic to return."

"You can't wait there! It wouldn't be safe for any woman. Have you got a friend you could stay with?"

"In Denver? I wouldn't call any of them friends . . . except for you."

Tap looked Rena straight in the eyes. "So why not stay in my room over at the Drovers'?"

"Are you invitin' me to your room, Tap Andrews? My, oh my, what is that spicy girlfriend of yours goin' to say?"

"Oh . . . well, I'll find somewhere else to bunk. And the good Lord willin', Pepper won't know anything about it. You need to pack some things, I presume?"

"Yes, but much fewer than you would imagine. I won't miss these dresses a bit. Grab me a valise out of the closet, would you? I got to find some other way to make a living than this."

Tap searched the closet and carried out a small black leather bag. "Well, you could always take in laundry," he joked.

A silk fringed pillow sailed across the room toward his head. "Laundry! I was thinking of opening a theater . . . oh, that's Vic's bag. I need the bigger one."

Tap dropped the bag and turned back to the closet. "I thought you said you were travelin' light."

"The big bag is travelin' light."

Tap tossed a large leather case on the bed. He stood near the south wall so he could watch Rena and the door to the room at the same time. As she folded and packed, Tap glanced down at Victor Barranca's leather suitcase.

"You think there's any chance Victor will be coming back here tonight?"

"I don't think so. But he will be back . . . or at least send Sarah back for some of his things."

"What belongs to him?"

"Well, that valise, for one thing. He calls it his 'possibles sack,' but I have no idea what's in it."

"Maybe it's time we looked." Tap walked over and picked up the leather bag.

"It's locked," she cautioned. "I don't have the key."

Tap slipped a knife with a six-inch blade out of his right boot and sliced a long hole in the side of the case. He dumped the contents on the bed.

"What are you lookin' for? A written confession?"

"Yeah, that would be nice."

Rena buzzed through the room stuffing a few more items in the large suitcase. "What did you find?"

"Marked cards, loaded dice, trinkets, bullets, a little pearl-handled, two-shot sneak gun, and a few letters . . . a Texas Ranger badge. Was Victor in the Rangers?"

"He stole it, no doubt. I think he was on the run from the Rangers when I met him in Mexico." She stepped to the bed. "A pearl-handled sneak gun? I don't remember seeing that."

"It looks a mite fancy for a man like Victor."

"I think I'll take that for my own. It's much less awkward than my .44."

Tap started to hand the gun to her, then walked over to the lantern.

"What is it?" she asked.

"It's engraved. 'For Col. C. Billingsly on his 50th birthday, Leland Stanford.'"

"Billingsly! It belonged to Billingsly?"

"Rena! This is it! It's the hard evidence the governor is looking for."

She picked up the small bundle of letters and sorted through them.

"Anything there?" he asked.

"Mainly clippings from newspapers."

"About what?"

"About the great outlaw, Victor Barranca," she answered. "And a dispatch from a Cheyenne bank."

"Victor has money in a bank?"

"As of the first of November when one thousand dollars was deposited in his name. How come he never told me about this? Wait . . . He didn't go to Cheyenne. He came in drunk about daylight and slept all day. I remember because we had a big party the night before, and he took off sayin' he wasn't about to wear a costume."

Tap glanced over at Rena. "When was Billingsly killed?"

"The last of October . . . that same day! The 31st, I believe."

"The next day after the shooting, a one thousand dollar bank account shows up."

"From the person who hired him?"

"Looks like it. But that's for the law to decide. We'll definitely take it to the governor."

By the time Tap had carried the valise down the stairs and Rena said her goodbyes, the Pearly Gate was just about empty. One card table still operated at the back of the room where five red-eyed men hovered between rags or riches. Two girls with emotionless stares still worked at the long mahogany bar.

One patron leaving in a small one-horse rig agreed to drop them off at the Drovers' Hotel. Hefting her suitcase to his second-floor room, Tap unlocked the door and lit a lantern.

"I'll get my bedroll and things."

"You know you don't have to go."

"And you know I do. First thing in the mornin' I'll take this sneak gun and bank letter over to the governor. Do you know what time the westbound train leaves?"

"I'll be goin' east," Rena informed him.

"East? I thought—"

"I've been thinking. Barranca will never go east. I'll head to Omaha. That train leaves at noon. I've got relatives in Delaware."

"Delaware? Well . . . anyway, I'll get you to the train."

"I could make it myself, thank you, but I would appreciate the help. Just in case Vic's around town."

"I figure Victor's on his way to Cheyenne with Sarah to collect that money."

"I don't think so. It's a letter of account. He would have to have that sheet of paper to collect the funds."

"So he'll be comin' back to the Pearly Gate!"

"And after that, comin' after me."

"Keep the door locked. Don't get yourself hurt."

"Thanks, Tap. It's been awhile since I had anyone care much about me." She sidled up to Tap. He still carried his bedroll and held his Winchester '73. Rena reached her left hand to his right shoulder and her right hand to his cheek. She pulled his head down closer to hers.

Suddenly Tap jerked back. "Rena . . . don't you go layin' that charm on me. I've made my decisions about the future, and I'm stickin' with 'em."

"Someday, Mr. Tap Andrews, I'm goin' to meet that Miss Pepper and see what it is that so captivates you."

"Maybe so," Tap mumbled. Then he opened the door. "Lock this behind me, and I'll be back in time to get you to the train. Maybe you can get some sleep."

"Sleep? You show up, and in less than twenty-four hours you completely rearrange my entire life. Now you want me to sleep?"

"Well, at least you're not bored," Tap replied sheepishly.

"Tap Andrews, since I met you in Globe City, there hasn't been one nice, peaceful boring day in my life."

He left Rena standing in the doorway.

The night manager signaled him from the front counter. "Will you be paying for two in your room tonight, Mr. Andrews?"

"Nope. I'm sleeping at the livery."

"Nice vest." The manager smirked.

Tap ignored the comment and plowed out into the night.

Lord, when I was in prison in Yuma, I used to think about get-

tin' out and findin' Rena. I was goin' to make her pay for runnin' out on me. But findin' her in the Pearly Gate . . . Lord, that's an awful place. She's been payin' for it, hasn't she? Anyway, You do what's fair by her, and keep me out of Arizona.

He reached the stable where he had boarded Brownie, and there he changed to his regular clothes. Then he traded the suit and vest to a blurry-eyed stable hand in exchange for sleeping in the loft, which was so full of winter feed that the only place to bunk was right at the top of the ladder. The air inside the barn was cold, and his bedroll felt like home. He closed his eyes and wished he could wake up at the ranch.

Tap wasn't sure why his eyes blinked open. It was already daylight, and the hairs on the back of his neck tingled with a strange anxious feeling. He had felt that way before. Grabbing his Colt and his Winchester, he leaped out of the bedroll and threw himself against the hay at the back wall of the loft.

The first bullet blasted through the boards from the stables below and punctured the lower end of his bedroll. The horses whinnied and danced in their stalls. His ears recorded each blast that shattered the hayloft floor; several danced his bedroll like a tin can target.

Ten shots. Two men with revolvers. One by the door, the other straight underneath. Barranca? No, Victor would have come right up here after me!

Deciding against the noise of cocking the Winchester, Tap pulled the hammer back slowly on the Colt and aimed for the top of the loft ladder.

"Did we get him, Benny? I can't hear nothin' movin'."

"Shoot, ain't nobody could live through that!"

"Well, go pull him down!"

"Fat Larry, you're closer to the ladder."

"What if he ain't dead?"

"Shoot him. Barranca don't care if he's dead or alive."

Barranca's behind this!

"What if it ain't him, Benny? We don't even know what this guy Anderson looks like."

"Andrews. His name is Andrews. The boy said the man who traded him the vest was sleepin' at the top of the ladder."

Tap glanced around and spotted a second ladder to the loft running up the rear wall of the building.

"Go ahead. Check it out," the one near the barn door called.

There was no reply.

He's sneakin' up the back way! I can't make any movement, or they'll make a sieve out of this floor.

Tap turned his Colt .44 toward the ladder up the back wall of the barn, the blued-steel sight planted at the head of the case-hardened valley.

If he comes up that center ladder, he'll get the first shot off. But if he comes up the back . . .

Suddenly the livery grew quiet. Even the horses seemed to hold their breaths. The crown of a dirty black felt hat crept into Tap's sights . . . then the whole hat . . . then a forehead . . . then dark, bushy eyebrows . . . Finally two narrow-set eyes glanced at the bedroll . . . then at Tap crouched against the hay.

"Well, I'll be a—" The man swung his revolver up.

Tap's bullet slammed into him. He plunged off the ladder and crashed to the floor below.

Tap rolled across the hay to the front end of the loft and came up with gun cocked and pointed where he had last heard the other man speak.

All he saw was a man running down the street away from the livery. He waited several minutes in case there were others, then crawled down the ladder, still carrying his cocked .44.

The gunman on the dirt floor was dead.

Tap found the stable boy cold-cocked on the dirt in front of the stable, wearing the fancy gold vest. A few splashes of water brought him around.

"My head hurts!" the boy complained.

"Yep. I imagine it does. Who were those two that hit you?"

"I ain't never seen them."

"How did they know I was up there in the loft?"

"I told them."

"What?"

"They was ridin' by early while I was hitching the Burnside rig, and these two ask where I got the vest. I told them I traded a man for it, and they asked where that man might be, and I pointed to the loft. The next thing I know, you was splashing water on my face. Are they friends of yours?"

"Nope. Sorry, son. Listen, me and Brownie are leavin' now. As soon as I'm gone, send for the marshal."

"Why?"

"He'll know what to do about that dead body in the barn."

"You killed one?"

"Yep."

"But I didn't even get to see the shootout! What do I tell the marshal?"

"Tell him exactly what happened."

"What did happen?"

"Two gunmen bushwhacked you, and then they tried to gun me down. I shot back. I have no idea who they are either."

"Who are you?" the boy asked.

"Nobody important."

Quickly saddling Brownie, Tap gathered his gear and rode through the nearly empty streets of Denver toward the governor's office. Though the early morning air was cold, he kept his coat unbuttoned and rode with his right hand resting on the handle of his Colt .44.

Barranca's out here somewhere—he and any other drifters he can enlist. The quicker I get out of Denver, the better. Pepper's right. Some towns are to be avoided. If we need supplies, we'll just roll the wagon up to Laramie. No more Denver!

Since the governor's office didn't open until 8:00 A.M., Tap reined up at a tiny cafe called the Rio Grande. Tying off Brownie in front of the restaurant's only window, he carried his rifle with him and selected a table in the back of the room where he could watch the front door and the window.

A man with a dirty apron walked over. "What'll it be, partner?"

"I'll take the biscuits, sausage and gravy, plenty of black coffee . . . and a clean piece of paper and a pencil," Tap replied.

"What was that?"

"You got a pencil and piece of paper in this place?"

"You writin' a dime novel, or will a scrap of wrapping paper do?"

"That'll be great. Thanks."

The steam rising from the hot gravy warmed Tap's face. Holding the blue-enameled tin coffee cup in his left hand, he began to write with his other.

Dear Pepper,

I'm writing because I'm not sure what's going to happen here in Denver, and there are certain things that you should know. I don't know if I can get the Arizona matter cleared up since I've spent all my energies trying to get Wade Eagleman out of jail.

Remember, I told you about the banker's wife down in Globe City? Well, I ran across Rena (that's her name) here in Denver, but I don't think she'll go back to Arizona and tell them what really happened to her husband. So I'm going to finish helping Wade and then come back to the ranch—and you.

Don't be jealous of Rena. When I saw her, I just had the strongest desire to hurry home and be with you. There's a lot of problems in our past that will haunt us 'til our dying day, I suppose. But we'll just have to face them together.

The Lord seems to keep you ever in my mind.

I like that.

Until we get to hold hands in front of the fireplace at the Triple Creek, I will remain faithfully yours,

Tap

"You makin' out your will?" a deep voice boomed.

Tap raised his Colt at the same moment he glanced up.

Then he grinned. "Stack! What in the world are you doin' in town still?" He shoved his revolver back into the holster.

"My baby sister was sick, and her husband's out haulin' freight, so I stayed a day or two extra."

"Can I buy you breakfast?"

"Nah. I already ate. You know how I like to cook my own eggs. Now what's this I hear about you?"

"I don't know. What do you hear?"

"One hundred dollars cash money for Tap Andrews in a gold vest, dead or alive."

"Barranca?"

"That's the rumor. I thought you came to Denver to clear things up. Seems like ol' Tap's just makin' things more involved. So what kin I do to help ya?"

Tap scraped up the last of his biscuits and gravy. "Well . . . one's easy, and one isn't so easy."

"I don't have to shoot no gunslingers, do I?"

"I hope not. Look, I want you to take this letter back to Pingree Hill and see that it gets out to Pepper at McCurley's."

"Letter? It looks like a scrap of brown wrapping paper."

"It's a letter. Trust me." Tap folded the scrap and handed it to Stack, who folded it again and stuffed it into his vest pocket.

"And the second thing?"

"I'd sure appreciate it if you would go over to the Drovers' Hotel and give a lift to a lady in room 24."

"A woman?"

"Her name's Rena, and she can help get Barranca arrested."

"A good-lookin' young lady, no doubt," Stack teased.

"Eh . . . well, yeah."

"Say." Stack stared at Tap. "This ain't no brush-off letter to Pepper, is it? I won't be a part of breakin' her heart, and you know it."

Tap laughed and finished his coffee. "Not hardly. But you can read the letter if you want."

"I don't read other's mail." Stack relaxed and took a deep breath. "So what about this woman?"

"Bring Rena over here to the Rio Grande, and then we'll go settle up with the governor. Rena's grabbin' the train east at noon. If all goes well with the governor, I might be able to roll out of town myself. It seems that maybe I ought to stay off the streets as much as I can."

"You're not plannin' to go down to Arizona then?"

"I'm plannin' to go back to the ranch, marry Miss Pepper Paige, and never leave home again. Doesn't that sound nice and peaceful?"

"Ain't nothin' peaceful about you or Pepper. Now what's the problem about this Rena lady in room 24 over at the Drovers'?"

"Problem?"

"You said it would be tough or somethin'."

"Oh . . . yeah, well, she used to be hooked up with Victor Barranca. And if he found her, he could be waitin' there for me to come back."

"So you're sendin' me into an ambush?"

"I hope not. Victor's not lookin' for you. Just take it slow, and if it looks sticky, pull yourself out of there pronto. You savvy?"

"You'll be here?"

"Yep. The governor's office doesn't open until 8:00."

"I'll go get her." He turned toward the door.

"Stack?"

"Yeah?"

"How's that baby sister of yours doin'? She feelin' better?"

Stack Lowery's smile extended from ear to ear. "Yes, sir, Tap, she certainly is. Thanks for askin'."

Stack walked out the door of the Rio Grande and disappeared.

Lord, it's men like Stack who keep this country runnin' right. It's not the politicians, railroaders, or the mining companies.

Tap was still drinking coffee when he saw Stack's loaded wagon pull up alongside of Brownie out in the street. Rena was blanket-wrapped beside him. Grabbing his rifle and with his boot heels banging on the wooden floor, Tap pushed the tall door open and was hit with a blast of cold air and a shout.

Thinking it was Stack calling, he tugged down his hat to shade the early morning sun and glanced up at the wagon.

"I said, are you that Andrews fella?"

Turning to his right, he saw a thin man with the top button of his overcoat tight against his Adam's apple and a Schofield Smith and Wesson .45 shaking in his right hand.

"Mister, don't be a fool," Stack called out. "Don't you know who you're holdin' a gun on? You've heard of the Arizona legend, haven't you?"

"Brannon? You're Stuart Brannon?" The man immediately released the hammer of his revolver and shoved it back into his belt. "Mr. Brannon, I didn't have any idea . . . It's my mistake. I thought you was a man named Andrews . . . Please, I ain't lookin' for no trouble. They told me you was this murderin' gunslinger, and I, eh . . . look, I'm leavin' here. My hands is up. You won't shoot me in the back? No, sir, I don't guess you would. Hope you have a nice trip back to Arizony . . . Yes, sir, I do!" He backed several steps down the wooden sidewalk, then turned, and ran around the corner of the dry goods store.

Tap looked up at Stack. "You sure put the fear in that old boy."

"He was already afraid. I just gave him some more reasons to be afraid."

Tap tipped his hat. "Mornin', Miss Rena."

"Mr. Andrews, I distinctly remember you promising that I could sleep in, and you'd be by about 10:00 A.M."

"Well, I didn't plan on Victor sending half the town out to shoot me. I figured you wouldn't be safe at the hotel."

"But the train east doesn't leave until noon. It looks like you're the one in danger."

"I think we'd both be safer waitin' at the governor's office."

"Well, I hope he has someplace I can catch some sleep," Rena replied. "You and your friends have been keepin' me up all night."

"Stack is a good man. I was the one who told him to go wake you up."

"No doubt. But I was referring to your lady friend."

"Who?"

"The one who beat on the door about six this morning."

"Who was it? I don't think I know any women in Denver still livin'."

"Stack, do you believe this man? I think he probably knows girls in every town west of the Mississippi, don't you?"

Lowery grinned ear to ear. "Yep. I reckon he does."

"Rena, don't get cute. Who was at the door?"

"How should I know? I was in my nightgown, so I told her to go away."

"You didn't even peek out to see who it was?"

"Well, she demanded to know if you were in the room, and I wasn't about to let her know."

"It must have been someone at the wrong room."

"Maybe you just forgot about this girl," she teased.

"Rena, I told you there's no one but Pepper."

Rena turned to Lowery. "Stack, you're a friend of Tap's. Is there really a yellow-haired darlin' that's agreed to marry him?"

"Yes, ma'am. Miss Pepper's a good friend of mine." Stack looked down at Tap. "You don't want to stand out here in the street all day, do ya?"

"Nope. Let's get over to the governor's office. Keep on the watch. Any one of these hombres might be tryin' to collect Barranca's bounty."

8

Pepper felt a little shaky. Her vision slightly blurred as she wobbled across the polished hardwood floor of the spacious guest room. She slipped out of the ball gown and hung it in the wardrobe closet. After pulling on her plain brown dress, she brushed back her hair and reset her ivory combs.

Then she stuffed her personal belongings into her bag and plopped it beside the dresser. She piled her wool coat on top of it and shuffled over to the blue velvet chair near the window. Slumping into the chair, she closed her eyes and rested her chin on her chest.

Lord, I'm goin' back to McCurley's. I'm not goin' to disappoint Tap like this anymore. I'm just goin' back no matter what happens. I don't know how I ever got into this fix. I've learned my lesson. No guilty conscience, no arm-twisting, no threats are goin' to make me risk losin' Tap. If I have to, I'll tell him about the baby.

He'll understand.

And . . . if he doesn't?

If he doesn't, I'll just die!

I wonder what's taking Rebecca Maria so long? Of course, I did tell her to find a rig on a very busy night.

Pepper flopped her head on the back of the chair and stared blankly at the ceiling.

To tell You the truth, Lord, I know I couldn't tell him. It would break his heart. The thought of it breaks my heart.

A gentle rap at the door brought her to her feet. She grabbed the back of the chair for balance.

"Rebecca Maria? Come in . . . come in!" she called.

The door pushed open only a few inches.

"Mrs. Dillard?"

"Governor!"

"With your permission, may I enter?"

"Oh, yes . . . of course. I would come to the door, but I seem to be a little dizzy."

The governor and his wife entered the room.

"My, what are you doing up, young lady? You should be resting." The governor's wife motioned toward the four-poster bed. "Let me help you."

"No—really I need to walk a little and get my legs back."

"We just wanted to check on you. I was so sorry to be interrupted earlier. A governor's time is never his own. Especially when there's a hanging scheduled."

"Oh." Pepper's eyes grew wider. "Rebecca Maria told me. What was the news that was so urgent?"

"It looks like we might have the wrong man in jail. I've postponed the hanging for a while."

"Governor, I was wondering." Pepper looked the short man in the eyes. "The man at the door earlier. I heard the voices in the hall. Is he someone from around here? I thought I might have recognized his voice."

"Oh, no, not from Denver. He's a rancher from up in the Medicine Bow country. I'd never met him before. I think he's a friend of Bob McCurley's. He's in town staying over at the Drovers' Hotel, so I suppose you could have met him somewhere."

The governor's wife stepped closer. "What can we do for you, dear? I had to enlist Rebecca Maria to help with serving. I'm afraid more people came tonight than expected. She mentioned doing you a favor but didn't say what you needed. Can we be of any service?"

"No . . ." Pepper looked to the floor. "Eh . . . well, this is a strange request. I really need some air. I was thinking of going for a walk, but as you can see, I'm a little woozy. So I wonder if you knew of a carriage available for just a short ride?"

The woman's face lit up. "Well, I think that would be a splendid idea. Fresh air certainly lifts my spirits."

"Yes, I'll tell Mr. Dillard, and I'm sure he wouldn't mind getting away for a short time," the governor offered.

"Oh, please, don't tell him," Pepper begged. "You see . . . eh, this party was so important for him to get to talk to all the different people about the railroad contract. I couldn't ruin his evening. If I might just do this on my own—Heaven knows, I don't want to cause him any more worry than I already have." She looked at the governor's wife. "I'm sure you know what I mean."

"I certainly do. You're right. We'll find a carriage, and you slip on down to the back door in the kitchen. I think a little crisp night air could clear your head and open your lungs."

"Thank you so much!"

"After all you've gone through," the governor assured her, "it's no bother at all. Give me a few minutes to arrange a carriage. Then come on down to the kitchen. And don't worry, it will be our little secret."

"You two have been very kind. I have appreciated all the gracious things you've done for me."

"Well," the governor said with a grin, "don't make it sound like you're leaving. Do plan on joining us for breakfast . . . that is, if you feel up to it."

Pepper hoped she would have no more visitors. After what seemed like a long wait, she slipped her coat over her shoulders so that she could fairly well conceal the valise in her hand.

At the top of the stairs she could hear the roar of the party in the ballroom below. A sweet aroma of perfume and punch drifted toward her as she quietly descended the mahogany staircase. On the platform at the bottom of the stairs, several men were involved in a heated debate, but none of them looked her way.

Quickly scooting toward the back of the house, she searched for a hall or door to the kitchen. She pushed a swinging door and found several women in bright white aprons arranging food on silver platters.

She stepped inside and waited a moment, trying to decide which of several doors led outside.

"Señora! I am so sorry." Rebecca Maria hurried over to Pepper's side. "The governor insisted that I help here for a while."

"It's all right. The governor said he'd get a carriage for me."

"You told him you were leaving?"

"I told him I needed some fresh air."

"Will you be okay? Are you going back to McCurley's? Was that your Tap Andrews who came by earlier? Make sure you take a carriage. Don't walk through the streets. You are not coming back, are you?"

"Whoa, Rebecca Maria. I'm going home. When Tap finishes his business, he'll come back. We'll get married and live happily ever after. And with any luck we'll never have to come to Denver again. Please do come and visit us at the Triple Creek Ranch."

"Maybe I will." Rebecca Maria looked around at the busy kitchen. "Do you want me to show you to the back door?"

"Yes, please. I don't want to run into Mr. Dillard."

"There's no chance of that. I saw him leave in a hurry a few minutes ago."

"Leave? You mean he left this party? But this was the whole reason for this charade, so that he could . . ."

"A woman with very long, dark hair came to the front gate with a note for Mr. Dillard. When he read it, I handed him his coat and hat, and he left."

Rebecca Maria took Pepper's arm, leading her past the pans hanging from the high ceiling and through another swinging door that seemed to lead into a large walk-in pantry. Pulling open a tall oak door, the maid stepped out into the brick courtyard pulling Pepper with her.

The cold night air hit Pepper, and she gasped and then coughed.

"Perhaps you should wait until morning?"

"No, no. I'm fine. I just need to get used to the cold."

"There is a carriage."

Pepper looked over through the darkened courtyard and saw the driver dozing off as he waited at the two-horse rig. With Rebecca Maria's help, she climbed onto the passenger bench. The leather seat radiated cold through her dress and coat, causing a chill to slip down her back.

"Goodbye, Señora."

"Thanks for everything, Rebecca Maria."

"Where do you want the driver to take you?"

"To Laporte or Fort Collins!" She laughed. "But the stage station will be fine."

"Nothing will leave until morning."

"In that case, I'll just find a corner by the stove and wait in the lobby of the stage lines. I'll be fine."

Rebecca Maria nudged the driver and gave him instructions. Amidst the clopping of the hooves on the bricks, Pepper waved in the dark at the maid.

She is such a kind woman, Lord. Reward her for the care she so freely gave me.

"Well, ain't this sweet!" the sickening voice of the driver broke the silence.

"Pardee?" Pepper groaned. "You're the driver?"

"Now isn't this a dee-light? Maybe we was destined to be together."

Pepper reached for her bag and fumbled in the dark for the catch. Pardee jerked the bag from her hands.

"Now there ain't no reason for you to go lookin' for a gun or knife. You might get yourself hurt! Just where do you think you're goin'?" he asked.

"Just where do you think you're takin' me?" she demanded.

"You've got three choices. I kin drive you out of town where Dillard is takin' care of some other business and see what he wants to do with you. Or I can shoot you right now and dump you over in some arroyo."

"What's my third choice?"

"Why, you and me can ride off to Texas and find a nice little cabin for the winter."

Pardee will kill me, Lord. He'll kill me . . . or worse!

"Take me to see Dillard," she demanded. "I want to see Dillard."

"Now that is a disappointin' choice!" Pardee reined up the rig and spit a wad of tobacco to the ground. Turning the carriage slowly around in the middle of the dark street, he slapped the reins on the rump of the lead horse.

Pepper lunged to the frozen mud of the roadway. She stumbled, tripped, fell to her right side, lifted herself up on her arms, and then scrambled to pull her feet underneath her. In the shadows she could see the carriage come to an abrupt halt. Junior Pardee's spurs jingled as he leapt to the ground.

Running to the darkened sidewalk, she sprinted along in front of a shop with no windows and turned down a narrow alley on the side of the building. She thought she could still hear the spurs in pursuit, so she held up her long dress and continued to run.

She paused long enough to button all the buttons on her coat and pull the wool hood up over her head. When she reached the next street, she turned to the right, and then turned left by a bakery with a light glowing in the back room and a sweet aroma filtering through locked doors. She stopped to catch her breath. Her left side splitting with pain, Pepper plopped down on the ground in an alley next to some empty wooden crates between two tall buildings.

She could hear her own gasps for breath.

She could hear her heart pounding.

But she didn't hear any spurs.

My bag is in that carriage—my money, my revolver, my clothes! Lord, what do I do now? I can't go back to the governor's. Pardee will watch for me there for sure!

I just don't understand how this happened! Everything I do complicates my life more and more. It's like I'm runnin' downhill and can't stop. Like that little boy in my dreams. Maybe that little boy represents me. I didn't think it would be this way. I mean, since I've begun to trust in You, Lord, I didn't think these things would keep on happening to me.

Pepper sat on the ground huddled against packing boxes until she dozed off. A few minutes later when she woke up, her toes ached with the cold; her cheeks and nose were numb; and her hands, which she had jammed into the pockets of her heavy wool coat, throbbed with each beat of her heart.

Standing to her feet, she walked cautiously out to the street. She felt dizzy and braced herself against the brick wall.

I don't even know what street I'm on . . . Nothing's open . . . The streets are almost empty . . . except for Junior Pardee. He's out there somewhere looking for me! You know, Lord, this would be an excellent time to wake up from a bad dream back in my room at McCurley's.

Lord, help me. I've really got myself messed up this time!

Pepper dragged herself along three blocks. She kept getting sleepier as she walked. Her feet throbbed with every step. Then she saw a dim glow from a large building across the street.

"The depot! The train depot! Thank You, Lord."

Pushing inside the lobby of the depot, she found at least two dozen men sleeping on the benches, chairs, and floor of the waiting room. A potbellied iron stove glowed at one end of the room.

Well, at least it's warm—crowded but warm.

The room smelled of alcohol, cigar smoke, and unwashed bodies.

"Sort of like the dance hall on a Sunday mornin'," she muttered.

A short man with a bushy gray beard, wearing a beat-up derby, struggled off the floor and staggered toward her. He leaned so close that his nose almost touched her cheek.

"Well, I'll be a . . . I'll be a . . . I'll be an Irishman! It's Veen Quick. I mean, it's Queen Vic herself!" he slobbered.

Pepper stepped back from the man. He again tottered toward her.

"I'm sorry to hear about your air dalbert . . . I mean, your dear Albert. My flamdolences to the conley."

Then he spun on his heels and shoved a sleeping man off the waiting room bench.

"Avast there, yon Phillips! Make way for the queen!"

The sleeper tumbled to the floor and continued to snore. Then the little man turned back to Pepper, bowed, and swung his hat in his left hand.

"Your hone, your thriness. Excuse the knave. He's a Welshman!"

"Eh, thank you, but I couldn't . . . ," Pepper began. Suddenly the old man toppled over backward and landed on an empty spot of floor in front of the door. He promptly rolled over, crushed his derby for a pillow, and fell asleep.

Pepper glanced at the empty bench.

Well, Lord, it's not home, but it's warm, and it is a place to sleep. Thanks.

When Pepper opened her eyes, it was still dark, but it had the feel of morning coming on. The heat from the wood stove had died, and the room was chilly but not cold.

I don't have any money. I can't go anywhere. . . . Rebecca Maria! Maybe I could slip into the governor's kitchen and get her to find my bag. Perhaps no one else will be awake.

Stepping carefully over the sleeping men in the train depot, Pepper buttoned her coat, pulled up the hood, and stole out onto the sidewalk. The daylight was just faint enough to see where to walk and read the store signs.

She ducked into the store fronts and alleys each time a carriage rambled down the street. Most of the early morning traffic seemed to be freight wagons.

A large carriage pulled by two black horses caused her to turn and quickly step inside the lobby of a hotel. She glanced back out the oval cut-glass window on the door as the carriage passed on by. It was then that she read the name on the door.

"The Drovers' Hotel?" she blurted out to the empty lobby.

Tap's here in this hotel! I can't let him . . .

She stepped back outside into the cold intending to run. But her feet wouldn't move.

Wait, maybe I could . . . couldn't I?

I could tell him I missed him dearly and came to be with him but lost my luggage on the stage. Or . . . someone stole my luggage! Yes, that's it.

But the McCurleys saw me leave with Dillard and Pardee.

I could tell them I got a lift with some old friends. Or I went to take care of some business, then came on to Denver to be with Tap.

But he'll ask me what kind of business.

Pepper pulled the hood down on her coat and unbuttoned the top button. She brushed some stray strands of hair back out of her eyes, but they flopped right back. Then she reentered the empty lobby.

Maybe I could tell him . . .

Lord, I'm just goin' to tell him the truth.

I'll tell him about Dillard.

About the baby.

Everything.

Well, maybe not the baby.

Pepper walked over to the registration desk. The guest ledger was closed, and there was no night clerk. But there was a sign: Please ring bell for clerk. She picked up a brass bell, then laid it back down. Swiveling the guest register toward her, she opened it and scanned the pages.

"'T. Andrews, Larimer County, Rm. 24.' That's Tap!"

She held on to the hand rail, pulled herself up the stairs, and shuffled down the hall to the room marked 24. She rapped lightly at the door.

I don't want to wake up the whole hotel.

The second rap didn't get a response either.

Come on, Tap. Please, be here!

Finally she banged on the door with the bare knuckles of her right hand. A woman's sleepy voice called out, "What is it? Who are you?"

Oh, no, I've got the wrong room!

"I'm sorry, ma'am. I understood this was Tap Andrews's room."

"Well?" the voice growled like the warning of a cat. "He doesn't want to see you."

"What?" Pepper choked.

"I said—"

"Do you mean to tell me this *is* Tap's room?"

"Go away, or we'll report you to the hotel management!"

Pepper was breathing short quick breaths, and she couldn't think of what to say next.

"Eh . . . eh," she stammered. "Open the door. I need to see him!"

"I will not open the door. You might need to see him, but he doesn't need to see you."

Pepper stood staring at the door.

No . . . no . . . Lord, no. Not my Tap . . . not like this! Please, Lord. Not him. Not him too.

Her mind blurred, and the tears streamed down her cheeks as she descended the staircase and found her way to the street. Scene after scene from her past flashed through her mind. Years of disappointing relationships and disastrous decisions rolled into view. She wandered right in front of a carriage.

The driver screamed something at her, but she paid no attention. As she was stepping up on the sidewalk, two strong hands grabbed her shoulders.

"Well, looky who I found walkin' the streets—jist like old times!"

Pepper turned to see Junior Pardee and another man behind her. She stared at them without expression.

"You don't look exactly happy to see us," Pardee bantered.

"And she ain't scratchin' your eyes out neither," the other man added. "Maybe that carriage accident left her, kind of, you know . . . touched?"

"Well, come on, Crazy Pepper. Dillard's waitin', and he's not a patient hombre." Pardee shoved her up into the back seat of the carriage and then climbed in after her. The other man crawled onto the front bench and took the reins.

The sun lodged between the eastern Colorado prairie and the clouds, creating a purple and orange sunrise as they drove southwest out of Denver. The wagon pulled in at an old stone house tucked off the road next to a cluster of leafless trees. Most of the windows were broken, and several were boarded over.

Half a dozen horses stood as sentinels in front, their breath fogging in front of them. Pardee helped Pepper to the ground.

"You ain't said nothin'. You ain't tried nothin'. If I was you, I reckon I'd be mighty worried about what Dillard might do."

He led Pepper into the stone house. The other man stayed outside with the carriage.

Daylight beamed through the broken windows to reveal Carter Dillard. He sat at a dust-covered table talking to several men. Jumping to his feet, he stormed toward Pepper. He grabbed her arm and yanked her close to himself.

"You're lucky I didn't have Pardee shoot you on sight. Don't you ever, ever think you can run away from me again. Now you listen, and you listen good. You and I are going back to the governor's office, and you'll stand at my side and smile when I sign that railroad agreement. Then we'll walk out of there, and Junior will take you back out to McCurley's. Have you got that clear?"

Dillard shook her with both hands. "Do you understand?"

"She ain't talkin', Dillard. She's touched in the head."

"Pardee, what did you do to her?" Dillard shouted.

"I ain't done nothin' . . . yet. She's touched, I tell ya. She didn't say one word all the way out here."

"Pepper!" Dillard shouted. "Don't you give me this silent routine! Pepper!"

Her mouth hung halfway open as she stared at a black-haired woman lying on the dirt floor in the corner of the room.

"She's just sleepin'," Pardee explained. He waved his hand only a few inches from Pepper's face. Without blinking, she continued to stare blankly. "See what I mean? Her head got busted, I tell ya."

Dillard released his grip on her shoulders and turned back toward the men at the table. "Junior, you take her outside. I'll be right there."

Pardee led Pepper to the doorway, then stopped, and turned to listen to Dillard.

"You understand?" Dillard was explaining. "After you bury the girl, you head out after Barranca. He'll try to get to Cheyenne to pick up that money. You plant him under, and it will mean $250 each."

"That ain't much for goin' against a guy like Barranca."

"There's four of you. He's not that good!"

"We'll go after Barranca, but we ain't buryin' no woman. We didn't shoot her. We ain't goin' to bury her." The others nodded agreement.

"Barranca used her for a shield. I didn't see any other choice," Dillard explained. "If you four hadn't been up all night at some dance hall, you'd have been out here in time to see that he didn't escape."

"When do we get paid?"

"When the work's done. Now get on up the trail!"

Pardee pushed Pepper outside to allow the four men to exit. They mounted quickly and rode to the north.

"Junior, I'll take Pepper to the governor's office and sign the papers. You and Milt bury this girl, whoever she is. Then meet me in town at the stage depot over on the west side. I'll need to get to San Francisco and talk to Crocker and Stanford. Then you two can . . . you know, take Pepper with you."

"Back to McCurley's?"

"Preferably not."

She didn't protest.

She didn't acknowledge their presence.

She didn't blink.

The cloud cover kept the morning bitter cold, but Pepper didn't bother pulling a blanket over her lap or even tugging the hood of her coat over her head.

Lord, he was my hope.

My only chance to be different.

It's not fair! I've spent my life around men who treated me mean. I just wanted one to love me. Only me. I wanted his thoughts to be on me when he gets up in the morning and on me when he comes to bed at night.

I wanted him to work hard to build our life together, dream about the future, and be able to forgive me for the past. I wanted to count on him like a rock . . . like a rock, Lord.

Dillard was saying something to her, but it was like a man outside a building shouting in. She didn't hear what he said.

She started to cry.

But this time there were no tears.

I don't know what to do, Lord. I really don't know what to do now. I don't have anywhere to go. That girl in the stone house was lucky. Nobody can betray her now. No one can treat her mean. Dillard will kill me too . . . or he'll have Pardee do it after they're through with me. I just don't care.

I don't want to try again, Lord. I don't have the strength. I give up. Heaven's got to be better than this.

And Hell can't be much worse.

She had no idea what time of the morning it was when they pulled up to the governor's office—maybe a couple of hours after daylight. Dillard had been threatening her about something.

What a jerk. If you're goin' to kill someone anyway, what good is a threat? Maybe I should just whip out a gun in the governor's office and shoot Dillard.

Pardee had returned her bag, but she could tell it was too light to contain her revolver.

Was Tap my special one? It don't matter. It's over between us. For good. Forever. I couldn't trust him. I can't trust any man.

Dillard led her into an anteroom outside the governor's office. He whispered something, but she couldn't understand what he was saying. They stood there for what seemed like a long time. Dillard made her pace the floor with him. Finally he stopped and rapped at the tall oak door.

The governor appeared.

"Sorry to keep you out so long, Carter. Oh, Mrs. Dillard, so glad to see you. I was afraid you might have gotten lost on our dark Denver streets. I assure you that will change soon. Yes, ma'am, the day is going to come when it's safe for a woman to walk in the dark on any street in Denver.

"I'm finally finishing up this hanging matter. We've caught the real culprit, and now I can pardon Eagleman."

"You what?" Dillard gasped. "You caught the real killer?"

"Well, we haven't apprehended him yet, but we just received some extremely convincing evidence. I've dispatched the sheriff to double the effort to capture him. It points to a despicable character, a hired gun by the name of Victor Barranca out of New Mexico. Or is it Mexico? Anyway, it's not Eagleman, and I, for one, am delighted to get him out of jail. Yes, I believe it was Barranca and some others perhaps. But enough of that. Mr. Whitney has the preliminary railroad contract papers spread across my desk. Shall we proceed to sign them?"

Dillard gripped Pepper's arm and strode into the office. She heard the governor say, "There're some folks here I'd like you to meet."

Tap tied Brownie off behind the wagon and crawled up next to Rena and Stack. Although they were only a couple of blocks away from the governor's office, he rested his hand on the walnut grip of his Colt .44.

"Keep an eye out on that side of the street, Stack."

"That fella Barranca surely has a mess of friends."

Rena clutched the top of her coat closed with her gloved right hand. "Not really. They'd happily shoot Barranca if someone offered enough money."

Stack parked the wagon in front of a half-built construction project diagonally across from the governor's office. The building looked like it had been abandoned until spring.

"Think I'll just keep an eye on things from here," he offered.

"You'll freeze," Tap warned. "You're welcome to come in with us."

"Not me. Talkin' to politicians and such ain't my style."

The governor was shuffling papers on his desk and talking to a heavy-set man wearing a dark suit and badge when Mr. Whitney led them in.

"Oh," Tap stammered, "look, if you're busy, sir, we can wait until—"

"No, Mr. Andrews, we were waiting for you. This is Sheriff Branger."

Tap tipped his hat.

The sheriff nodded. "Andrews? I think I heard of an Andrews down in New Mexico . . . Or was it Arizona?"

"This Mr. Andrews is a rancher from up in the Medicine Bows." He turned to Tap. "I'm afraid we haven't been able to apprehend this Barranca fellow yet. Did you find anything that will help us?"

"Yes, sir, I think we did." He pulled the small engraved handgun out of his pocket and laid it on the governor's desk.

The sheriff picked up the gun and studied the engraving. "This looks like Billingsly's. Look at this!" He handed it to the governor. "It was the one old Stanford gave him. Where did you get this?"

"In Barranca's valise."

"Did you find anything else?"

"Only this." Tap handed the wrinkled telegram to the governor.

"One thousand dollars in Cheyenne? I don't understand."

Tap pointed to the date. "The day after Billingsly was killed, someone put a one thousand dollar line of credit in a Cheyenne bank in Barranca's name."

"Looks like someone hired him!" The sheriff held the telegram at arm's length so he could read it.

"Well, Victor Barranca's not the type to shoot someone for a wallet and a pocket watch."

"The two of you will need to sign a statement certifying that you found these items among Mr. Barranca's personal effects."

"Yes, we will." Rena nodded.

The governor slammed a fist on the oak desk. "We've got him now! This is quite incriminating."

"Barranca's worried. He's sent more than one man to kill me in the past few hours."

"What?" the governor gasped.

"You've got a body over in the west side livery, Sheriff. Two men tried to jump me there. And another tried in front of the Rio Grande."

"My word!" The governor shook his head.

"Are you sure Barranca's behind all that?" the sheriff asked.

"Yep. The word in the saloons is that Barranca will give any man one hundred dollars for killin' me."

"We have to apprehend this Barranca with utmost dispatch. Sheriff, will you take over this search immediately?"

"If he's in this county, we'll have him by nightfall. Now if you'll excuse me." He pulled his dark felt derby back on.

"Tell your men to be careful. Barranca will draw against you. And he's good," Tap cautioned. "He wears that .45 on his left side and has a cross-body draw."

The sheriff looked Tap up and down. "You know a lot about shootin' for a cattleman."

"I went up against him in the Pearly Gate last night. It's fresh on my mind."

The sheriff exited through nine-foot doors on the window side of the office.

Tap turned back to the governor. "What about Wade Eagleman? Can he be released yet?"

"Mr. Whitney?"

"Well, technically he can only be released by a pardon from you, Governor."

"By all means, get the papers. Let's get this matter settled."

"It's not that easy, Governor. With a pardon, it means Eagleman remains convicted of the crime. A pardon doesn't change that conviction. Therefore, we can't try the man Barranca for a crime that has already produced a conviction."

"Hang the formalities!" the governor huffed. "I'm giving him a pardon. Let the attorneys figure out how to try this Barranca fellow. Maybe we'll get him to confess. Then we don't need a trial. My word, Whitney, this is Colorado, not New York!"

"Yes, sir—"

"And get the statements for them to sign."

"Yes, sir."

When all the paperwork was completed, the governor turned and shook Tap's hand.

"Mr. Andrews, the state of Colorado certainly owes you a great thanks for keeping us from hanging an innocent man."

"Wade's a friend of mine. It's the kind of things friends do for each other." Tap shrugged.

"Your loyalty is admirable."

"Why, Governor, you sound like it's an election year," Rena softly chided.

"Mrs. Andrews, politicians are always running for office. It's in our blood, I suppose."

Tap winked at Rena. "Actually, sir, Miss Rena is not—"

A heavy rap at the door interrupted them.

"Oh . . . I forgot! I have an important appointment. Go ahead and process those papers, Whitney. I'll get the door."

Tap couldn't tell who was in the hall, but it sounded as if the governor was greeting old friends. The governor popped back into his office. Nodding at Tap, he beamed. "I've got some folks here I'd like for you to meet."

Suddenly the couple stepped through the doorway, and Tap looked straight at them.

"Mr. and Mrs. Dillard," the governor announced, "this is Mr. and Mrs. Andrews."

9

Pepper?"

"Tap!"

"Oh, splendid!" The governor smiled. "I see you all know each other. Well, Carter, let's step to the desk and finalize the railroad matters." He pulled Dillard on into the office.

"What are you doin' here?" Tap tried to control his voice, but the end of the sentence was twice as loud as the first.

"Perhaps you'd like to visit in the rotunda?" The governor nodded toward the door.

Rena, still attached to Tap's arm, led him out to the waiting room in front of the governor's office. Pepper stormed out behind them, slamming the door on the governor of Colorado and Carter Dillard.

"What am *I* doin' here?" she huffed. "What's the matter? Didn't you plan on gettin' caught?"

"Who is that man you were with?"

"Who's he? Who's that saloon girl holding on to your arm?"

"Is this your little Pepper?" Rena purred.

"Little Pepper? What dance hall did he drag you out of?"

"Mrs. Dillan! He called you Mrs. Dillan!" Tap shouted.

"Not Mrs. Dillan. Mrs. Dillard."

"Well, are you?"

"What?"

"Mrs. Dillard?"

"Of course not! And you . . . how about you—good, old faithful Tap Andrews! Is this Mrs. Andrews?" Pepper screamed.

"No! You know me better than that!" Tap shouted back.

"Know you better? Know you better? For all I know she's not even the same one who was in your hotel room all night!"

"My hotel room? You secretly followed me to town to see who was in my hotel room?"

"I didn't follow you to town! I didn't even want to come to town! Oh, God." Pepper began to sob. "I don't even want to be here right now."

Rena sidled up even closer to Tap. "Well, you're here, girl, so you better explain."

"Shut up and get away from him!" Pepper demanded.

Suddenly Mr. Whitney appeared and pushed his way between them. "You'll have to carry on this . . . discussion outside, I'm afraid. You've completely disrupted the governor." He ushered them to the outside door even as their argument continued.

Pepper shoved Rena away from Tap as she passed by. Swiftly Rena grabbed a hank of Pepper's hair, pulling it loose from the combs, and held on. Furious now, Pepper slammed a tight right fist into Rena's midsection, causing her to lose her grip. A second blow was intercepted by Tap who stepped between them.

"What are you doin'?" he demanded.

"I want to talk to you alone, Tap—right now!" Pepper cried.

"This is the lady of your dreams?" Rena howled.

"Pepper, I want to know who—"

"Get rid of her, Tap!" Pepper screamed.

"Who was that man!" Tap hollered.

Pepper was sobbing, and she could feel herself losing control. "Why did you have to be a woman-chaser? I can't live with that, Tap!"

"Me? I'm gone from home two days, and you run off with some peddler."

"He's not a peddler."

"Tap, take me to the depot. I don't intend on standing here and gathering a crowd," Rena insisted.

"Shut up, or you'll be drawin' buzzards!" Pepper bawled.

A man's voice cut through the argument. "You two look like you need help."

"Stack!" Pepper cried out. "Take me to April's!"

"Well . . . if—"

"No!" Tap hollered. "Take Rena!"

"To April's?"

"No, take her to the wagon."

Rena tried to protest, but Stack led her by the arm across the street.

Pepper was near hysterics. "I hate you, Andrews! I hate you! Of all the men I've hated in this world, and I've hated a lot, I hate you the most! The rest were all jerks. But you . . . you deceived me. You broke my heart."

"Me? What in the world are you talkin' about? I came here to get things taken care of. You knew exactly where I was and what I was doin'. I came here to try and settle up that mess in Arizona."

"It looks to me like you came to take up where you left off in Arizona. Next you'll be telling me that she's the husband-killin' darlin' that you went to prison for."

Out of the corner of his eye, Tap noticed a crowd starting to form on the sidewalk around them.

"Well, for your information, Rena *is* the lady from Globe City. But what difference does that make?"

"Oh, no. It don't make any difference to you. Anyone wearin' a dress will do."

"How dare you accuse me like that? I suppose sneaking off and pretending to be another man's wife is just a parlor game to pass the time away."

A short man in a tight suit pushed his way through the crowd. "I'm afraid you two will have to move along. It's quite inappropriate for you to—"

"Stay out of this!" Tap shouted. "It's no concern of yours."

"But I must insist!"

Pepper grabbed the man by the lapel of his coat and jerked his head close to hers. "He said to stay out of it!" she hollered, shoving him so hard that he stumbled back into the crowd.

Turning back to Tap, Pepper brushed the tears from her green eyes with the sleeve of her coat. "The truth is, you came to Denver just to chase women. Admit it!"

"I'll admit nothin'. But I'll tell you somethin'," Tap shouted, "if I wanted to chase women, I certainly wouldn't come to the governor's office to do it! You never once asked me what I was doin' here."

"Ask you? Ask you? I was in the governor's office too. You heard them talking about a big railroad deal. What do you think that's all about? Or are you so sure of yourself you don't need any facts? The mighty Tap Andrews doesn't need the truth. Any old lie will do!"

"Facts? The truth is, God knows I've done absolutely nothing immoral with that woman . . . well, not since Globe City. And here you are livin' with some man pretendin' to be his wife."

"We might have stayed in the governor's house, but I didn't live with him. I've been true to you, Tap. I've been true to you, and you let me down!"

"How in the world is staying with some man in the governor's house being true? You don't even know what bein' true is!"

Tap felt his face flush red. He was so angry he had to stop and catch his breath. At that moment Dillard pushed his way through the crowd. He marched up to Pepper and grabbed her by the shoulders.

"Do you realize what you've done?" he shouted. "You've ruined the whole railroad contract! The governor has backed out. He wants to think about it some more . . . think about it. Do you know what that means? I've lost the whole deal. You just cost me hundreds of thousands of dollars! You'll pay for this. Believe me, you'll pay for this royally!" Dillard grabbed her arm and started to drag Pepper through the crowd.

Tap spun him around with his left hand and caught Dillard with a right uppercut to the chin. The sound of knuckles hitting chin cracked as loudly as a freighter's whip.

Dillard staggered back and fell to the ground. "Mister, I didn't like you on the trail, and I surely don't like you now. But don't you ever, ever touch her again!" Tap growled. "Or it will be your last act on this earth!"

Tap turned toward Pepper and laid his hand on her arm. "Are you all right?" It was the first soft word he had spoken to her.

She nodded and whispered, "Yes."

A murmur from the crowd caused Tap to whip around. Dillard, still sprawled on the ground, pulled a short-barreled .38 out of his pocket. The toe of Tap's boot caught him on the fleshy part of the inner wrist just below his coat sleeve. He let out a curse and dropped the revolver. With one motion Tap grabbed the man by the coat collar and yanked him to his feet. Drawing his Colt .44 with his right hand, he shoved the cold steel barrel against the man's temple.

"You'll regret this!" Dillard shouted. "You have no idea who I am. I'm happen to be—"

Tap shoved the barrel of the gun into the man's blubbering mouth and cocked the hammer. "Yeah, I know who you are. You're the man who had the top half of his head blown off in front of the governor's office."

"Pepper . . . Pep . . . st- . . . stop him!" Dillard mumbled.

"Why?" she asked quietly.

Two badged deputy marshals waded through the crowd. Both carried short-barreled shotguns.

"Put the gun down, mister!" they hollered at Tap.

"Glad you men came along. He drew on me," Tap explained. Then he put the hammer back down and removed the gun but kept it in his hand.

"Arrest him! He was about to kill me!" Dillard shouted.

"Who drew on who?" the deputy asked.

Several in the crowd shouted, "The one in the suit. He drew on the other man first."

"Dillard went for his gun."

"This old boy is jist protectin' hisself!"

The deputy grabbed Dillard by the arm. "The rest of you get on out of here. Then he turned to Tap. "That goes for you and her too! And I don't want to find you stirrin' up trouble in some other part of town neither. If it happens again, I'll be draggin' you off. *¿Comprende?*"

Tap holstered his revolver and cradled Pepper in his arm. It was a gentle touch that she hadn't felt in several days.

"Where do you think you're takin' me?" she demanded.

"Somewhere we can shout and yell and not draw a crowd."

Neither spoke as they walked across the street toward Stack and Rena who waited next to the wagon.

Stack stood there with folded arms shaking his head. "Most nights at April's are pretty tame compared to you two."

"Look, Tap, you and that bobcat can scream and yell all over this town, but I want to get to the train depot. In case you forgot, Vic Barranca is lookin' to kill me," Rena put in.

"She really is the Globe City woman?" Pepper asked again.

"I see I have a reputation. It doesn't matter. I cried all those tears a long time ago."

"You want me to deliver her to the depot?" Stack offered. "Deliver! Pepper! Tap gave me a note to give you. I guess I might as well deliver it to you now."

Pepper unfolded the note and began to read it to herself.

Tap Andrews, if this is a goodbye note, I'm goin' to kill you on the spot.

Dear Pepper,

I'm writing because I'm not sure what's going to happen here in Denver, and there are certain things that you should know. I'm not sure . . .

She stopped reading for a moment and brushed back the tears. Then she studied each word.

. . . the Lord seems to keep you ever in my mind . . . hold hands in front of the fireplace . . . faithfully yours,

Tap

Oh . . . Lord, what if . . . what if he didn't? What if I've been the one?

Pepper turned away from the others and looked at her feet, her chest heaving with sobs. Strong hands gently rubbed her neck and shoulders, then slipped down around her waist, and pulled her close. Pepper leaned against Tap's chest. His lips brushed against the hair pulled behind her right ear.

"Let's go talk," he whispered. "We got to figure this thing out before we die of worry."

"Look, I'm talking about my life here!" Rena intruded. "Get me to the train!"

Tap walked to the back of the wagon and began to unhitch Brownie.

"Stack, you know that big favor you once said you owed me?"

"Yep."

"Well, now I'm collectin'. Swing by the jail, and if Eagleman's not released, tell him he will be soon—if all this yellin' hasn't messed that up too. I'll meet him over at his office later today. Then take Miss Rena to the depot and stay with her until she boards the train. But be careful."

"You want me to wait around town for you two? We could all ride back to the mountains together."

"Don't wait for us, Stack. Only the good Lord knows what we're goin' to do next."

"If you two are comin' back by Pingree Hill, stop in for a visit and some eggs." Stack tipped his hat, slapped the reins, and rolled out into the street.

Tap turned to Pepper.

"I can't think very good in cities. Can we go for a little ride? Let's rent a buggy."

"Brownie will do just fine. Help me up."

Tap laid his hands on Pepper's waist and lifted her to the saddle. She scooted back of the cantle and perched on his bedroll.

Tap patted the horse. "Put your head down, Brownie." Then he swung up in front of Pepper. She pulled the hood up on her coat and slid her hands around his waist.

"Keep your eyes peeled. More than one person's tried to shoot me today," he cautioned.

"There's worse things that can happen," she warned. "I figure

Dillard won't rest until he gets even with me. He knows I'm stayin' out at McCurley's."

"Yeah, I shared some coffee with him on the trail, but I never thought he was goin' to see you. What were you doin' with him anyway? I hope your explanation is easier than mine."

"Easier? I'll die havin' to tell you. Wait 'til we get someplace private-like. You and me will both need to sit down for this one."

Tap steered Brownie out to the west of town, past some plowed fields to Clear Creek. The sky remained overcast and heavy, but it had neither rained nor snowed, though the creek showed signs of freezing near the bank. He eased Pepper to the ground, then dismounted. Loosening the horse's cinch, he allowed the gelding to graze the short dead grass that lapped out from the creek.

Without saying anything, Tap scouted around for some dry sticks and soon had a small, hot fire blazing. One log too big for the fire was rolled over as a bench. He motioned for Pepper to join him.

He sighed a big, deep sigh. "Well, where in the world should we begin?"

"You're goin' to have to start . . . 'cause I really don't think I can tell you everything without breakin' down," she admitted.

"Why is it we're now sittin' here peaceful-like talkin' this over? Less than an hour ago we were yellin' and screamin' hateful things for the whole town to hear. What made the difference?"

"You goin' after Dillard, I guess. Tap, he's been blackmailin' me for days, and I couldn't get away. You've got to believe me. I tried! I ran, and they caught me. I prayed and prayed for the Lord to save me. And there you were—backin' him down. No matter how much you hated me, you'd still back him down."

"I don't hate you."

"You will."

Tap took a long stick and scratched at the fire. "Tell me what it's all about."

"You've got to tell me first," she insisted.

"Where do you want me to begin?"

"How about that jade who was in your hotel room all night?"

"I wasn't there. I was sleepin' at the livery."

"She said you were there!"

"She lied then."

"Well, she didn't exactly say . . . ," Pepper reflected. "But she didn't mind me believin' you was there."

"I was busy shootin' some ambushers. That you can find out easy-like. There's a kid with a big bump on his head who will tell you what happened."

"Maybe you should start from the beginning."

"You mean, when I stopped to see Stack at April's or when I got to Denver?"

"Start with April's. Why did you stop to see Selena?"

"No . . . I said I stopped to see Stack," Tap contended.

"And I say you must surely have visited with Selena."

"Okay." Tap grinned. "I'll start at April's."

Actually, he started at the campfire where Dillard and another man named Pardee first pulled off.

Thirty minutes later they were standing with their backs to the fire when he finished.

"That's why we were at the governor's office. We had some proof about Barranca, and the governor decided to pardon Wade Eagleman."

"But why did you need to pretend to be Mr. and Mrs. Andrews?"

"We didn't. The governor just assumed that, and he never listened to me try to explain it. Rena's afraid to go back to Arizona so the only thing I accomplished was gettin' Wade off the hook. Now . . . some of it sounded strange, I know, but you've got to believe me 'cause it's the truth . . . and 'cause you know that I love you. Pepper, you've got to trust me. I don't go lookin' for trouble, but all my life it seems as if I'm in one scrape after another."

"I believe you, Tap. I believe you because your story is easier to swallow than mine."

"Do I get to hear it now?"

"I'll tell you as much as I can. Where do you want me to begin?"

"Begin with explainin' why this Dillard was blackmailin' you."

"I think," Pepper said softly as she turned and sat back down by the fire, "I'd better start before that."

Pepper spent almost the next hour explaining the ordeal of the past several days, describing the trip to Hot Springs, the wagon accident, the governor's house, the night at the depot, the shock of finding a woman in Tap's room, the capture by Pardee, the dead girl in the stone house, and the anger in discovering Tap and Rena arm-in-arm at the governor's.

Still poking at the fire and looking down, Tap slipped his arm around Pepper's shoulder.

"Now you told me everything . . . except what it was Dillard had over you," Tap pressed.

"I told you I was nearly dead one time, and he paid for nursing me back."

"But what were you sick of? I mean, it sure does seem a whole lot deeper than just a generous man helpin' a sick girl."

"I can't tell you, Tap." Pepper began to cry. "I want to tell you. I want to believe that it won't make any difference. I really want you to love me no matter what . . . but I can't tell you. I just can't!" she sobbed. "I thought I could do it . . . but I can't . . . I'm just too ashamed . . . Don't ask me . . . Please, don't ever ask me!"

Tap stood her to her feet and held her tight with both arms wrapped around her shoulders. "It breaks my heart to see you hurt so much," he finally said softly. "But I'll wait. Someday . . . when it's the right time. I really want . . . I need you to tell me. But I'll wait."

"But it might be a long, long time," she whispered.

"I've got time. I'm not goin' anywhere but home."

"Take me back to McCurley's, Tap. Let's leave right now."

He cinched up Brownie, stomped the fire out, and then swung into the saddle, pulling Pepper up behind him.

"I've got to go back to town. I've got to make sure Wade, Stack, and Rena didn't run into trouble. If Barranca's runnin' around lookin' for me and this Dillard and others are lookin' for you . . . well, who knows who they will shoot at. A man's got to stick by his friends, Pepper."

"Even if it means he gets shot?"

"Yep."

"Why? What's the purpose in that?"

"Well . . . you know . . . It's a part of the code. It's just . . . the way I am. You understand, don't you?"

"Tap, I've spent most of my life around people that don't give a hang about me, let alone stand up for me. You and Stack are just about the only ones."

"Well, that's a good reason. Let's go make sure that long-legged piano player is on his way safely back to April's."

As they rode toward the western outskirts of Denver, an occasional snowflake drifted out of the clouds.

"What have you been thinkin' about?" she asked as they slowed Brownie to a walk.

"Barranca was paid big money to shoot the railroad man Billingsly. But who gained anything by his death? Your friend, Dillard, moved in to try and snag a railroad contract. Is he the one who hired Barranca? Have we been lightin' the fuse at two ends of the same stick of dynamite?"

"Maybe that's why Dillard got all jumpy when the governor said he was releasin' Wade Eagleman," Pepper added. "One of them will be huntin' the other down, don't you suppose?"

"If they don't find us first." Tap turned back in the saddle. "Are you as cold and hungry as I am?"

"Yes, but I want to get out of Denver as soon as possible."

"That makes two of us. If all went well at the depot, we should catch up with Stack before he makes Longmont. We'll travel with him as far as April's."

"You did visit with Selena, didn't you?" Pepper quizzed.

"I stopped to see Stack, but she wandered downstairs, and I had to say hello."

"She wants you, you know."

"Selena wants a man who will treat her nice—that's what she wants."

"Don't we all? But let me tell you somethin'. I've been thinkin'. The next time I catch a woman hangin' on your arm, I'm goin' to shoot her dead on the spot!"

"How come I only attract gun-totin' women?" He laughed. "That doesn't sound like the Christian thing to do."

Pepper was silent for a moment. "You're right. I shouldn't have said that. Next time I find a woman hangin' on your arm, I'm goin' to forgive her for her many sins."

"That's better."

"Then I'm going to shoot her!"

Tap pointed several blocks up the street. "Looks like lots of folks waitin' for the train. We must have gotten back before it pulls out. Maybe Stack will still be here."

He looked back at her and winked. "'Course, it just might be some old boy and his girl arguin' at the top of their lungs. I hear that will draw a crowd in this town."

Pepper held him a little tighter. *Lord, I got a feelin' every once in a while me and Tap is goin' to fight like cats and dogs. It's the way we are. Now I'm not makin' excuses, but I just wanted You to know ahead of time so it wouldn't surprise You none.*

She glanced up the road at the train depot. "If everyone is waitin' for a train, how come they're standin' out in the middle of the street?"

Tap rode Brownie to the back of the crowd and called down to a bushy-bearded old man with tobacco stains across the front of his coat.

"Hey, professor! What's the commotion?"

"Reckon, I cain't say, but there was a rumor that Queen Victoria was in town last night."

Pepper nudged Tap. "Remind me to tell you about that sometime. Look . . . there's a man, a Spaniard or Indian, waving at you." She pointed across the crowd to the edge of the wooden sidewalk.

"That's Wade Eagleman!"

Tap slipped down out of the saddle and helped Pepper to the ground. After looping Brownie to a black iron hitching post, they pushed their way toward the arm-waving Eagleman.

"Wade, you old Comanche! It's good to see you out on the street," Tap shouted.

A pained look broke across Eagleman's face. "Tap, I don't

know all you had to do, but you did it. I owe you a big one. But, look, things went bad here."

"What happened?"

Wade pulled Tap back against the bakery wall behind the crowd. Pepper stepped back with them.

"Eh . . . Wade, this is Pepper. The girl I'm goin' to marry."

"Pleased to meet you. Tap and Stack told me lots about you."

"Is Stack still here?" Pepper asked.

"Stack and that Miss Rena picked me up at the jail. I rode down here to the depot with them, figurin' you'd show up here, and I could give you a proper thanks.

"Well, we had sat here about an hour when guns started poppin' out on the platform. Near as I can figure, Barranca was out there—"

"Victor's here?" Tap asked.

"I guess Barranca was hoping to slip out of town on a train when four gunmen opened up on him. One of them clipped him in the leg, but he leaded two of them to the ground. Most folks in here pushed back away from the window and waited.

"Then with guns still blazing, he busted into the lobby and spied Rena. He took aim at her, and she froze. Before I could do anything, Stack reached out to grab her . . . and that big, old boy took her bullet."

"Stack got shot!" Pepper cried.

"Yep. He fell. Everyone stampeded for the doors, and I tried to grab Rena. Barranca threw a couple shots back at the two men still chasing him, and then he fired at me. I dove behind a bench. Shoot, Tap, I just got out of jail, and I'm not carrying a gun. When I peeked around the corner, he was dragging Rena up the stairs to the storage room."

"What happened to Stack?" Tap asked.

"I drug him out and laid him inside the bakery here and sent for a doctor."

"I'll go check on him," Pepper called as she ran to the front door of the bakery.

"And Barranca?"

"Well, the deputies showed up and arrested the two still alive that jumped Barranca. But Victor's up there in the storage room with Rena, demanding that he and her be the only passengers on the next train out. He threatens to kill her if anyone comes up the stairs."

"What are the deputies doin'?"

"Waiting for the marshal to get here, I suppose. Tap, what can we do? I think he really will kill her if anyone gets too close."

Lord, I got Rena into this, and I've got to get her out. If I can't take care of my friends, I'm worthless.

Tap went over to Brownie and pulled an extra revolver from his bedroll. He tossed the Colt to Eagleman, who checked the chambers and slipped a bullet out of the side of Tap's bullet belt.

Most of the crowd stayed halfway across the street from the railroad station. Only a deputy and a man with a black silk tie hunkered down outside the depot door with its recently shattered glass panes.

"Better get down," the deputy shouted. "There's a killer up there."

"You boys look like you could use an extra hand. Mind if we help out?"

"Appreciate it. But I can tell you right now, I don't like goin' up against the likes of Barranca, no matter how many men we have."

"I've gone against him before," Tap told them.

"And you're still alive?"

"Last time I looked in a mirror." Tap peeked through the broken glass into the depot. "Is there any other way into the storeroom besides that door up at the top of the stairs?"

The man with the black silk tie cleared his throat. "Yes, sir. A double swinging door opens out toward the tracks."

"Is there a block and tackle at the top?"

"Yes."

"Is the door locked from inside?"

"I can't really say . . . normally it's not locked. I mean, no one can use that door from the outside anyway. But there is an iron bolt on the door. The gunman could have locked it."

"But the door opens out—not in?"

"That's correct."

"What do you aim to do, mister?" the deputy questioned.

"Why don't you two divert him while Wade and I try to figure how to get up in that door and flush him out?"

"Divert him? You mean give him a target to shoot at?"

"Nope. Just get him talkin'. Promise him somethin'. Keep him busy."

"Promise him what?"

"Eh . . . promise him . . . promise him that you got a train on the way, and it will be ready for him in a half hour."

"What good will that do?"

"It will keep Rena alive for at least a half hour and give us some time to figure how to get up through that door."

Tap and Wade Eagleman crouched below the window and crawled along the side of the building to the south. Then they worked their way to the tracks. Tap could hear the deputy and the station manager shouting something to Barranca.

Pausing at the corner of the building, Tap whispered, "Which leg took the bullet?"

"The right one, but he still made it up those stairs."

"Raise me up on the block and tackle real slow. But we can't have that thing squeak, or I'm a dead man. From now on, talk to me with signs. We won't be able to say a word out loud. You haven't forgotten how to talk sign, have you?"

"White man's humor falls on deaf ears of stoic, noble red man," Wade teased.

"Go on. I hope you're prayed up," Tap encouraged him.

"Waiting around in jail to be hung gives a man plenty of time to pray," Eagleman assured him.

Strapping the rough, inch-thick hemp rope around his waist, Tap signaled for Wade to begin the pull. With his left hand holding the rope for balance, Tap clutched his Colt .44 with his right. Keeping the gun always pointed to the loft door, he inched his way up the side of the depot.

The movement was slow, and Tap grew impatient. He fought the urge to speed Wade up, knowing any noise at all would alert Barranca.

Finally coming even with the unpainted wooden door, he swung his feet around to brace against the framing board at the bottom of the entrance. With his left foot in place, he gently lifted his right foot—and caught his spur on the depot's Denver sign. His spur jangled like a doorbell at a mercantile. He heard movement inside the loft.

Shoving sharply to his right with his left foot, he clutched the shingled roof eave on the right side of the opening with both hands and tried to hold himself there without swinging back in front of the doors.

A bullet blasted through the wooden door where Tap had just been hanging. His grip starting to loosen, Tap watched as five more shots shattered the door. One of the bullets hit the hemp rope, breaking several strands. The rest looked as if they might snap at any moment.

Then what was left of the door flew open, blocking Tap's view of who was inside.

10

Still clutching the Colt and hanging on to the shingles at the same time, Tap felt his grip on the roof beginning to slip. He kicked the door violently with his left foot. The bullet-pierced loft door slammed into Barranca's right hand, causing him to drop the revolver to the loading dock below. He staggered back and stumbled over some packing crates.

Tap pushed off from the depot wall, trying to swing to the loft opening on what was left of the hemp rope. He could see Barranca struggle to get to his feet. Clutching the side of the loft wall, Tap felt the rope snap. He dropped his Colt and clung to the rough, unpainted door framing, his body dangling down the side of the depot.

Bowie knife in hand, Barranca crawled toward him, being careful not to give those below an open shot. He slashed at Tap's right hand. There was a sharp, fiery pain as blood gushed out. Instantly jerking his right hand back, he found himself suspended by only the grip of his left hand.

Barranca lifted his knife to strike again, but Rena pounced on his back clutching his arm with both hands. The gunman rolled over trying to loosen her grip. Tap slapped his wounded hand up to the casing and struggled to pull himself into the loft.

Rolling onto his knees, he tried to brush off his throbbing right hand and succeeded only in smearing blood over his bandanna and face. Pulling a knife out of his boot with his left hand, Tap dove at Barranca who had just sliced through the upper left sleeve of Rena's coat. She leapt back clutching her arm.

Barranca labored to his feet and faced Tap. Both swinging knives, they jockeyed for position. Blood oozed from Barranca's leg wound, and Tap felt the desperate need to stop the bleeding in his hand.

They spun one circle. Barranca dropped to his right knee, and Tap dove for him. Barranca came up with a short two-by-four in his left hand and slammed it into Tap's right wrist just above the wound. The pain was so sharp he dropped the knife to grab his arm, and at that moment Barranca lunged his knife at Tap's stomach.

Jumping out of the way, Tap kicked wildly at Barranca's wounded left leg. When the boot connected, Barranca let out a scream and rolled to the floor, dropping both the two-by-four and the knife. Finding his right hand useless, Tap caught him in the cheekbone with a left cross. Barranca's head jerked back and slammed into the floor, but his knee caught Tap in the stomach. Staggering to his hands and knees, Tap found he couldn't breathe. Rolling to his back and gasping, he saw Barranca seize a knife and start toward him.

Just then the storage room door burst open. Victor Barranca turned and threw the knife at the gun-toting deputy in the doorway. The deputy jumped to the side, and the knife struck him in the upper left shoulder. He dropped to his knees and squeezed the trigger on his drawn revolver.

The first shot caught Barranca at the base of his sternum. With a look of shock, he staggered back toward the open loft door. The second shot hit him in the left chest area, and he tumbled backwards out the open door, plunging to the platform below.

Rena ran to Tap's side and helped him to his feet.

"Tap! You're covered with blood!"

Bending at the waist to regain his breath, he labored to talk. "It's not . . . not that bad . . . really . . . my hand . . . Pull off my bandanna, would you?"

Finally able to breathe again, he stood straight and wrapped his burgundy silk bandanna around his wounded hand.

"Rena, are you cut?"

"Just my coat."

"He didn't hurt you before we got here, did he?"

"Not much. Thanks for coming for me."

"Well, Victor won't be hurtin' anybody anymore."

"Nope, and I'm grateful for that."

They walked over to the deputy. Several men were helping him to his feet.

"Partner," Tap began, taking a deep, labored breath, "you crashed through that door at the right time. How you doin'?"

"I'll make it," the deputy replied. "How about you?"

"This?" Tap looked at his bloody hand. "I've cut myself worse than this eatin' tough meat."

"Mister, thanks for helpin'. Say, I don't even know your name."

"Call me Tap. But it don't matter. When they start grabbin' women for shields, it's time for every man to make a stand. You'd better get that knife wound to a doc."

"And the same for you."

Tap dusted off his hat with his left hand and punched it back on his head. Rena walked with him down the narrow stairs. Wade Eagleman met them at the bottom, handing Tap back his Colt.

"Sorry I couldn't help more. When you were up there scuffling, I was afraid of shooting you or Rena by mistake."

"Rena's safe. That's the main thing. And she won't have to worry about Barranca stalkin' her. Look, I have to check on Stack. Would you wait with her until her train gets here? I suppose they will get back on schedule now that the excitement is over."

"I'll take care of her," Wade assured him.

"Rena, be nice to Eagleman. You never know when you'll need a good lawyer."

"What about the Arizona thing?" Wade Eagleman asked. "I still want to help you clear up that matter."

"Don't worry about it now. I just want to get Stack and Pepper and ride out of Denver. I'll write you. Maybe you can ride out and spend a few days at the ranch . . . if all the passes aren't snowed in."

Rena squeezed Tap's arm. "I'd kiss you on the cheek, Tap Andrews, but you've smeared yourself with blood. I can't figure out if you're the toughest, tender man or the tenderest, tough man I've ever met."

"I'd like to invite you to stop by and see the ranch too, but . . . well, I don't think Pepper would approve."

Rena gave a knowing smile and took Wade's arm. The two retreated into the train depot waiting room where some sort of order was being restored.

Tap scooted through the dispersing crowd, most of whom stood and gawked at his blood-smeared face. Pepper ran to meet him in the street.

"Tap! Are you shot?" she cried.

"Nope."

"But you've got blood all over you! I heard gunfire."

"Barranca's dead."

"Did you . . ."

"No. It was one of the deputies that brought him down."

"But . . . the blood?"

"I took a knife blade in the back of the hand, and I guess I smeared it all over me. It burns like anything, but I can get that sewn up. How about Stack?"

"The doc said it looked like the bullet busted a collar bone and then passed on out. He figures it will heal without much problem providin' it don't fester up. He surely won't be playin' the piano for a while."

"Or drivin' that wagon back. Is the doctor still with him?"

"I think he went over to the depot."

"I'll check on Stack. If you find the doc and he isn't busy, send him back over here. I'm goin' to have to eat and shoot left-handed for a few days."

"I'll go find him. Are you sure you're all right? You're a mess!"

"Go on before you get all smeared up too."

Pepper scooted across the street.

Stack was sitting on the floor of the bakery with his back against the wall. He was shirtless. Clean, white linen bandages were wrapped all over his chest, shoulder, and arm. With his left hand, he was eating a fresh-baked biscuit about the size of a horseshoe.

"I came in here to give my respects to a dyin' man, and there you are all dressed out and eatin' a hole in the bakery," Tap jibed.

"Me dyin'? Look at you! What's the matter? Wouldn't death take you until you got cleaned up a bit?"

Both men quit smiling about the same time, and their eyes turned serious.

"You doin' okay, Stack?"

"It'll be stiff for a long time, but I'll survive. Where did you take it?"

"I just got knifed in the back of the hand."

"But it's all over your face."

"That's what I heard. I kind of smeared it around."

"There's no kind of to it. You're a mess." Stack grinned.

"Thanks for takin' that bullet for Rena."

"You'd have done the same thing. Sometimes a man don't have time to think. Some things you've just got to do. You know what I'm talkin' about."

"Yep. You think you'll be up to ridin' in that wagon of yours?"

"You drivin'?" Stack asked.

"Yeah. I thought Pepper and me would see you back to April's. The girls can take care of you there."

"That would be mighty fine, Tap. Mighty fine."

"Rest there a little longer. I'm going to step in the back and find myself a basin of water and try to clean myself up. Pepper will be along with a doc, and I'll get him to sew me up. It might snow before dark, but I think we ought to roll out of town as soon as you are able."

It was almost an hour before Tap had his hand repaired, his face clean, and Stack loaded under some blankets in the back of the wagon. Tying Brownie behind the wagon, Tap climbed up into the seat with Pepper. He slapped the reins left-handed.

"This is like a hospital wagon," he quipped. "Pepper's got a knot on her head. I've got a bandage on my hand, and Stack is wrapped up like a stick of dynamite went off in his vest pocket. Don't we make a sight?"

As Pepper spread a blanket across their laps, he glanced back at Stack. "Boy, we sure had a good time in Denver, didn't we?" he teased.

"Tap, if it ain't too insultin', next time I think I'll just come and visit my little sister by myself."

"Sounds mighty boring, Mr. Lowery—mighty boring."

"Yeah. That's what I like about it. Being around you, Andrews, is like being caught in a tornado. Sometimes a breezeless day can be mighty peaceful."

"Speakin' of breezes, do you feel that east wind startin' up?"

"Yeah. Sort of feels like a chinook, don't it?"

"That's what I was thinkin'."

"Well," Stack called out, "the passes ought to be open then."

"And muddy!" Tap added, as he turned around to pay more attention to the driving.

The afternoon warmed dramatically as the southwest wind blew the clouds away. In less than two hours, they had assigned the blankets to the back of the wagon, unbuttoned their jackets, and pulled off their gloves. The wagon wheels began to throw mud, and Tap could feel the team pulling hard to keep the rig from sliding.

"How long will this warm weather last?" Pepper questioned, digging into the bakery bag and handing Tap a large bear sign.

"Maybe a day or two. . . . Then one of those cold winds will blow down from Rupert's Land and drop temperatures by thirty or forty degrees."

Pepper turned back to hand a roll to Stack. "He's asleep," she said to Tap.

"It's a good day for it. I was thinkin' of doing the same thing myself."

"Why don't you crawl back there by Stack and rest?" Pepper suggested. "You've lost a considerable amount of blood. I can drive the wagon awhile."

"Listen, you're the one with a nasty bump on the head. You need the rest as much as I do."

Pepper slipped her arm into Tap's. "How's your hand feelin'?"

"It hurts! But as long I don't bust out these stitches, I'll survive. Besides, I can still wiggle my trigger finger."

"I think you ought to go back to the ranch and stay there until the weddin'."

"So you think we ought to go ahead with it then?" he teased.

"The sooner the better, Andrews. If I'm not out there at the ranch lookin' after you, you'll just get into more trouble."

"Me? How about you? Why, I can't even leave you at McCurley's without you wanderin' off."

They both sat silent.

Tap felt the warming breeze in his face and squinted at the glare of the slightly declining sun.

"I guess we better not continue the direction of this conversation, had we?" he finally admitted.

"I suppose we'd just end up yellin' at each other."

"That would wake up Stack."

Pepper sighed but kept holding tight to Tap's arm. "It will be nice to live at the ranch. We can yell all day and not bother the neighbors."

"You suppose we'll have days like that?"

"Reckon so, don't you?"

"Yep." Tap leaned over and brushed a gentle kiss across her temple. "Tell me about the weddin' plans."

"I thought we were waitin' until you solved that Arizona business."

"I changed my mind."

"Well, in that case I've got an idea or two."

Tap pulled the wagon way off the side of the road to allow a fast-moving, mud-tossing stagecoach to gallop past them. "Go ahead—what have you got planned already?" He put the wagon back into the center of the road.

"It's got to be a small wedding. We'll hold it out at the ranch . . . on Christmas Eve."

"Christmas Eve? That's only a month or so away!"

"Oh, you can wait that long, can't you? Anyway, Bob McCurley said he'd give me away, and, of course, we'll ask the reverend to do the honors. Christmas is on a Monday this year. Did you know that?"

"Well . . . eh, no, I guess I never thought about it."

"Anyway," Pepper continued, "I want Danni Mae to be my maid of honor, and I thought Stack could be best man . . . if that's all right with you. I mean, if you wanted to have someone like Wade Eagleman, I'd understand."

"Stack will do just fine."

"I figure you'll want to invite some of the boys up on the Rafter R, and I want to have some of the girls from April's. Is it all right if I ask some of the girls to come?"

"Not *all* the girls? Does this mean that Selena has to stay back at the dance hall alone?"

"Well . . . I might invite her. She can just sit there and eat her heart out."

"That's mighty neighborly of you."

"And I'm going to make me a cream-colored wedding dress and you a shirt to match."

"Cream? Not white?"

"Tap, you know I don't deserve a white dress . . . but the Lord's forgiven me for all that. Your shirt will have a high collar and sort of ruffles down the—"

"No ruffles! Absolutely no ruffles!"

"I knew you'd say that. I just knew you were goin' to hate the ruffles."

"Well, you're right."

"Okay, no ruffles. Anyway, I want to decorate the house with pine boughs and cedar, and Stack can play the music on the grand piano since neither you or me can make a decent note with it. Did you know Danni Mae can sing? Well, she can. She was a singer in New York City. Then she moved west with a man named Percy. He dumped her in Central City. Nice guy, huh? I met him one time, and he seemed like a decent fellow, but you never know by lookin'."

"What's she goin' to sing?"

"Who?"

"Danni Mae."

"Oh, yeah. Danni Mae will sing 'Amazing Grace.' Is that all right with you?"

"Yep."

"Then after the service, we'll have a sit-down supper. I thought we could have the wedding about 2:00 P.M. That way we can have supper and send everyone home early."

"Why would we want to send everyone home?" he teased.

Pepper's elbow cracked into his ribs so quickly that he jumped to the side of the wagon seat.

"Come back over here."

"Are you goin' to clobber me again?"

"Sooner or later."

"I think there's a stage stop hotel up there on the top of that next pass. How about calling it a day and gettin' a fresh start in the mornin'?"

"Sounds good to me." Pepper yawned. "I surely didn't get much sleep last night." She released Tap's arm and scooted over on the wagon bench. She tried to pull her hair back up in the combs.

"Is that it?" a voice from the back of the wagon rumbled.

Tap glanced back. "Stack! What do you mean, is that it?"

"I been back here faking to be asleep, and all I see is one little peck on the cheek that looked like you was a visitin' your old maid aunt."

"Boy, you've been hangin' around those dance halls too long!" Tap quipped.

The conversation continued light through supper at the small one-story roadside hotel. The sun had set, and Stack had retired when Pepper suggested a walk.

"It's still mild out there. It might be the last decent evening 'til spring," she reasoned.

They hiked up the hill west of the hotel. At first the setting sun was blinding, and they tramped slowly. Pepper held on to Tap's arm with her right hand. Her left hand lifted her dress up out of the mud. Soon the sun dropped behind the Rockies. They stopped to get their breath and survey the road and hotel below.

"Aren't these chinooks something? Within hours the temperature shot up thirty or forty degrees."

Pepper took a big deep breath and stretched her arms out. "It's wonderful! You know, everything always looks and feels so much better when you're out on a hillside. Do you know what I mean?"

"Yep. You can see things clearer. Both the things around you and the things in your mind. I could never live in a city like Denver."

Pepper turned back and studied the dark shadow of the snow-capped mountains. "I lived in Denver for a while once."

"When was that?"

"Oh, a few years ago. Remember, I mentioned when Dillard helped me. I only stayed there about . . . nine months or so. I didn't like it at all."

"Why in the world did you live in Denver?"

"Oh, me and April had a big argument, so I went to Denver. But, like I said, I didn't stay long."

They walked along the ridge toward the south for a few moments. It was Tap who spoke first.

"I guess . . . you and me . . . There'll always be secrets for the other one to discover."

Pepper nodded. "There are just some things too horrible and embarrassing to mention to anyone."

"Well," Tap continued, "this is the way I figure it. The Lord knows all about every one of those sins in our past. And He knows our weaknesses now. Plus He understands what we will face in the future. Right?"

"Yes."

"And knowin' all that, He figures you and me can make it anyway."

"God's never wrong."

"So . . . we're stuck with each other."

Pepper started to poke him and then remembered the bandanna wrapped around his right hand.

"How's your wound?"

"Let's take a look." Tap pulled off the stained bandanna and held up his hand. "Stitches still look pretty good. And it's not puf-fin' up. Actually, it's doing better than I thought. Mainly it's just stiff."

He glanced at her, and she seemed to be staring right through him. "Pepper? What is it?"

"Oh . . . I was just wonderin'. How many times over the years will I have to look at your fresh wounds?"

"It's a wild and rugged land, Pepper. Until it settles down, there'll be some rough, hard people. Some of them will be rogues. Some of us will have to make a stand against them. Ever since I began to believe, I've determined that my stand is going to be on the right side."

"I know. It's the way I want it really," she added. "It's just that I worry about some drifter shootin' you in the back."

Tap grinned. "I'm not Bill Hickock or someone like that. Just a small-time cattle rancher from northern Colorado."

"Well, come on, Mr. Small Time. We better get down the hill before dark."

Tap pulled her back with his left hand. "Wait a minute! Come here."

"What for?"

"Do you know how this day started?"

"Eh . . . I was in the train station sleeping on a bench in the mid-dle of a bunch of drunks."

"And I was in a hayloft being shot at. Then we spent the morn-ing yelling and hating each other and the noon hour in a fight at the depot."

"Not to mention being kidnapped, threatened, and knifed. It wasn't boring. Is that your point?"

Tap shook his head. "Nope. My point is we've been so busy we've neglected the most important thing of all."

"And what's that, Mr. Andrews?"

Tap slipped his left hand on the back of her waist; his bandaged right hand cradled her blonde hair.

Pepper closed her eyes and felt his warm tender lips press against hers. When he finally pulled back, her eyes popped open.

"Yeah . . . well . . . maybe we don't have to get back to the hotel so quickly."

She threw her arms around Tap's neck and kissed him long and hard.

Lord, let there be a whole lot more times like this and a whole lot fewer times like this mornin'.

It was totally dark by the time they returned to the hotel. They stood for a moment outside Pepper's door.

"What time are we pullin' out in the mornin'?" she asked.

"I'll get up early and get the rig hitched up. A lot depends on Stack. If he needs more rest, maybe we'll take a little extra time."

"If the chinook's blowin' still, we could go for another walk."

"Now look, lady, do you really like the exercise, or are you just tryin' to get me alone on that hillside so you can kiss me on the lips?"

"Wouldn't you like to know!" She batted her eyes and slipped inside her room.

Tap collapsed in the bed and slept so deeply that he didn't wake up until almost daylight. Stack snored away, so Tap dressed quickly and scooted out of the room. He tried not to make too much noise with his jingling spurs and thumping boot heels.

Carrying his Winchester in his left hand, he grabbed a tin cup of coffee from the hotel kitchen in his right and backed his way out the door, strolling out into the yard in front of the hotel.

The warm chinook wind still drifted up from the southwest. The skies were so clear he felt he could reach up and touch the snow-capped Rockies. To the east the sun had not yet risen, but an orange glow on the horizon signaled that it was only moments away.

Tap stopped by the corrals and looked over the horses. Leaning the rifle against a post, he sipped his coffee.

Lord, this is like August—not November. Last August I was sweatin' down in Yuma at the Territorial Prison. That was a lifetime ago. Almost like lookin' back on a different person. Well . . . I am a different person. I did a lot of dumb things in the past, and

I'll have to live with the consequences. Just help me not to do dumb things in the future.

Thanks for a new day . . . and a new chance.

"Well, Brownie . . . let's go home. Onespot will be missin' you, and Sal will be tired of eatin' nothin' but mice. I'll grab that tack, and we'll get you suited up for the day."

Balancing the empty tin coffee cup on the top of the corral post, Tap stepped into the shadow-darkened barn.

The first blow struck just above his shins. It felt like an axe handle or rifle barrel. Falling to the dirt, he reached for his Colt but felt the cold steel of a revolver crash into the side of his head.

Trying to roll out of the way, he managed to get his hand to his holster—only to find it now empty. Protecting his injured right hand, he defended himself with his left hand. He warded off one kick to the face but took hard blows to the stomach and kidney. Gasping for breath, Tap made it to his hands and knees and then felt something slam hard against the back of his head. He collapsed face-first in the dirt, straw, and manure of the barn floor.

Catching his breath and adjusting his vision to the darkness, he felt someone yank his hands behind him and tie them with a leather strap.

"He don't look like much now, does he, Dillard?"

Tap could feel blood trickle into his left eye from a wound inflicted by a kick in the head. Even with his hands tied, he rolled over and tried to prop himself up against a barn wall. Through blurred vision he saw Junior Pardee approach him with a carbine in his hand. He raised the barrel, and Tap braced himself for yet another blow.

"Leave him alone, Pardee!" a deep voice shouted.

Pardee spun toward the other man. "What difference does it make if he's awake or cold-cocked? You're goin' to kill him anyway, right?"

"It makes a lot of difference. I want him to know who it is that outsmarted him!" Carter Dillard stepped into sight.

Tap fought to get his breath as he strained at the leather straps that held his wrists. "Dillard!" he panted. "I should have known it would take a soft-skinned coward to bushwhack a man, tie him up, and then shoot him."

Pardee started to swing the carbine barrel at Tap's head, but Dillard shoved him out of the way.

"I said no!"

Suddenly Pardee spun and pointed the carbine at Dillard. "Don't you ever, ever shove me again! You understand?" he screamed.

"I pay the bills around here, and you'll do as I say!" Dillard yelled back. "And I say he needs time to think about the fact of who it is that is doin' him in."

Pardee continued to hold the gun on Dillard.

Tap felt that the leather straps on his wrists might be loosening. "Pardee, what's a gunman of your quality doin' workin' for such a pasty-faced swindler like Dillard?"

"He pays good."

Dillard ignored Pardee and walked up close to Tap. "You insulted me in front of the governor. You lost me hundreds of thousands of dollars. And you thought you were just going to ride out of town? No one lives long who crosses Carter Dillard!"

"Yeah, you tie them up and shoot 'em. Now that ought to make you feel like a brave man."

"Don't try that line on me because when I'm through with you, I'll put a bullet through your head without another thought."

Pardee turned back to face Tap. "Where's Pepper?"

"How would I know?"

"She seemed to think you were the heroic type who'd come rescue her, and now you're the one needin' help. We heard she and some crippled-up piano player were travelin' with you."

"I'm by myself."

"You're a liar!" Pardee sneered. He kicked wildly, but Tap rolled out of the way of the blow.

Dillard pulled back the hammer of his revolver and aimed it at Pardee. "Back off, Junior! I'm settlin' this right now!"

Pardee pointed the carbine at Dillard. "Maybe this is the time to settle plenty of scores!"

With Dillard and Pardee faced off, Tap pulled his left wrist free from the leather straps.

The sound of a rifle being cocked at the doorway of the barn caused all three men to stare at the shaded figure standing in the morning light.

Pepper had watched daylight creep into the hotel room through curtains so thin she thought it prudent to get up early and dress while it was still partly dark. By the time she could see the yard outside the hotel, she had her hair pulled back and set in combs.

I'm goin' to get back to McCurley's and sit in the bathtub for three days. Then I'm goin' to put on my fancy dress and sit in the parlor until Christmas. Christmas! The wedding! I'll have to get that dress made and Tap's shirt . . . maybe just a few ruffles.

I wonder if he's up yet? He's probably out with the team. Maybe he'll walk up on the hill with me, and maybe we could . . .

Pepper carried her coat on her arm down the hall and out into the dining room. Someone from the kitchen staff was straightening tables. She waved as she stepped outside onto the narrow, covered porch. Strolling out toward the corrals, she held her hands up to shade her eyes from the rising sun. Something on the fence post caught her attention.

A coffee cup? A rifle? That's Tap's '73 with that long-range sight! He's up already. Maybe he's in the barn.

Laying her coat on the rail next to the coffee cup, she picked up the rifle and walked to the barn door.

I'll tease him about leavin' this out here.

Hearing shouts come from inside, she paused at the door. The voices were too familiar. Without another thought she shoved the door open. Cocking the .44-40, she stepped in holding the heavy rifle to her shoulder.

"Pepper!" Tap called out.

"Well, ain't this a quack!" Pardee sneered with the carbine at his hip but now pointed toward Pepper. "I jist been thinkin' about you, missy."

"Pepper, put the gun down before I have to shoot you," Dillard commanded.

"You ain't goin' to shoot her," Pardee barked. "You wanted Andrews. Well, you got him. Me . . . well, after we lead the lover-boy down, I think me and Miss Pepper might just ride down to Texas for a spell."

She pointed the rifle at Pardee, then at Dillard, then back at Pardee. Both men began to move slowly at her.

"You come any closer, and someone's goin' to get shot!" she hollered. Then with a slight tremble in her voice she cried out, "Tap, are you all right?"

"I'm not exactly my handsome self," he called. "If you're going to shoot one, shoot Pardee!"

She whipped the rifle back toward Junior Pardee, and he instantly stopped moving toward her.

"Pardee's a fair shot, so shoot him first. Aim for the gut. Now Dillard couldn't hit a buffalo from five feet! Isn't that true, Pardee? Dillard's just a blowhard that's always hired someone else to do all the work. Isn't that something, Junior? He gets the money. He gets the women. He gets the fancy clothes, and some other poor sap has to do all the work!"

"Shut up! He's just stallin', Junior. You kill the girl; I'll kill Andrews!" Dillard hollered.

"Yeah, that's it!" Tap roared. "He kills the guy who's tied up and wants you to take the first round of that 200-grain lead bullet."

"I said, shut up!" Dillard spun toward Tap and kicked at his head. As he did, Junior Pardee lunged and grabbed the barrel of Pepper's rifle. At that moment Pepper squeezed the trigger, and the blast bounced the rifle off her shoulder. She staggered back.

Junior Pardee was lifted off the ground by the impact and flew back about five feet. For a moment he stared in disbelief at the bullet hole just below his rib cage. "She done killed me!" he moaned and then slumped to the dirt on the barn floor.

Tap, having just freed his other hand from the leather bindings, caught the toe of Dillard's boot with both hands and, twisting it hard, brought the man crashing to the ground. Pouncing on his back, he shoved Dillard's arm behind him and kept him pinned face down in the dirt. Both men stared over at Pepper and Pardee.

Pepper threw the rifle to the ground and slumped down to a sitting position against the barn wall.

"Pepper? Are you hurt?"

"I think I'm goin' to vomit," she called.

"Put your head between your knees," Tap called out. "Quick. Get your head lower!"

"It's not the first time she ever pulled a trigger!" Dillard cried out.

Tap increased the pressure to the man's arm.

"But then there's probably a lot of things she's never told you," Dillard mocked.

Pepper wanted to shout something. She wanted to pick up the gun and shoot Dillard. She wanted to grab Tap and get him out of there. But all she could do was gasp for breath and try not to pass out.

"Look, Andrews, you got a right to know what you're gettin' there!" Dillard continued. "Ask her what she owes me. Ask her about how I saved her life. Ask her about what I did for her and the baby."

"NOOOO!" Pepper began to sob.

Tap rolled Dillard over and caught the man with a left cross to the head and then three quick upper cuts to the chin. On the third cracking blow, Carter Dillard's eyes rolled back, and he slumped unconscious to the dirt.

Tap crawled over to Pepper and pulled her head to his chest. He could feel the blood on his face mat in her hair, but he held her tight.

For several minutes he rocked her back and forth. Tap could hear horsemen gallop off the road and into the hotel yard. Finally he pulled back and lifted up her chin so that she would have to look him in the eyes.

"It's all right now, darlin' . . . it's all over," he tried to soothe her. "It's all over. You saved my life. It's all right."

"But . . . it's not all right . . . what Dillard said—"

"In the barn!" a deep voice bellowed from outside. "This is the county sheriff! I want you to walk out right now with your hands in plain sight. Do not carry any firearms!"

"Come on, Pepper-girl. Sounds like the posse arrived a little late. Let's go over to the hotel and clean up."

Tap left his rifle and Colt lying in the dirt and helped Pepper to her feet. When he stood, his right knee gave out on him, and he put his arm around Pepper's shoulders. They limped together to the barn door and shoved it open.

The county sheriff and a dozen posse members sat on their horses with guns drawn.

"Andrews! My word . . . Have you been shot?"

"We're okay, Sheriff Branger."

"We tracked Carter Dillard and Junior Pardee here. Cheyenne telegraphed to say that it was Dillard who deposited that money in Barranca's account. I'm to arrest those two for instigating the murder of Billingsly."

"They're inside," Tap reported, still limping with Pepper toward the hotel.

"Are they dead?" the sheriff called.

"Maybe Pardee, but Dillard's just knocked out."

The sheriff and his men dismounted and cautiously ran into the barn.

"Pepper . . . wait a minute . . . Let me catch my breath."

"Tap . . . I can't talk about it. I wouldn't blame you one bit if you wanted to leave me, but I can't . . . I just can't talk about it." She began to cry again.

"Pepper, look at me! Don't look down. You got nothing to look down about! I love you . . . I don't care what it is you can or can't tell me. It doesn't make any difference."

"It would if you knew," she sobbed.

"Nope. It's done and over. Now sometime when we're about sixty and sittin' on the porch, and the grandkids run back down to their house, and you feel like talkin' . . . well, then you can tell me all about it if you want. Whether now or then, it just doesn't make any difference. Ten minutes ago in that barn I thought I would never feel you in my arms again. It was the most dead, empty feelin' I've ever had. Then there you were at the door! As soon as I saw you there, I knew everything would be all right. That's the only thing that matters."

Pepper stared into his brown eyes. "Do you mean that?" She stood on her toes to kiss him but then pulled back.

"You don't have a clean place on your whole face! You look as bad as yesterday!"

"I aim to fix that up shortly. Let's go home, darlin'."

"Hey . . . Andrews!" the sheriff called out from the barn door. "What happened in here?"

"Me and Pepper—we stood them down, that's all. Didn't we, girl?"

"Yep. We stood 'em down."

The sheriff walked toward them. "Say, you are plannin' on coming back to Denver to testify, aren't you?"

"Nope. Let the dead bury the dead," Tap replied. "But you can come out to the ranch, and we'll sign a testimony. Now we've got a weddin' to plan, and I'm not leavin' the Medicine Bows again until we've said those vows."

He smeared his coat sleeve across his mouth.

"Hey, Pepper-girl, I think my lips are clean now." He turned and gave her a wink.

For a list of other books by
Stephen Bly
or information regarding speaking
engagements write:

Stephen Bly
Winchester, Idaho 83555